A GENIUS AT THE CHALET SCHOOL

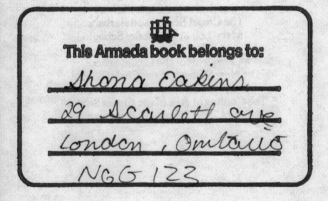

A GENIUS AT THE CHALET SCHOOL

ELINOR M. BRENT-DYER

This book contains Part I of
A Genius at the Chalet School
first published in 1956.
Part II is available in Armada in *Chalet School Fête*

Armada

A Genius at the Chalet School was first published in
the U.K. in 1956 by W. & R. Chambers Ltd., Edinburgh.
This revised edition was first published in Armada in 1969 by
Fontana Paperbacks,
8 Grafton Street, London W1X 3LA.

This impression 1983

Printed and bound in Great Britain by
William Collins Sons & Co. Ltd., Glasgow.

CONTENTS

Chapter		Page
1.	NINA MAKES A STAND	7
2.	ADVENTURE ON THE TRAIN	15
3.	NINA HEARS THE NEWS	26
4.	THE FIRST NIGHT AT SCHOOL	37
5.	SETTLING IN	51
6.	PREFECTS IN COMMITTEE	64
7.	TROUBLE!	80
8.	MARY-LOU SEEKS ADVICE	94
9.	JOEY PUTS A FINGER IN THE PIE	103
10.	"BEAUTY AND THE BEAST"	110

Chapter I

NINA MAKES A STAND

SIR GUY RUTHERFORD sat glaring at the schoolgirl sitting at the other side of the table with a good deal of impatience. She glared back and there was furious indignation in the dark eyes that fronted him.

"I wish you'd hear reason!" he said suddenly. "You're—how old? Fifteen, isn't it? Very well, then. You're still at an age when what you need is school and a jolly good school at that!"

She straightened herself. "There is no need," she said. "I have read and I mean to go on reading. But at my age, and if I'm to make music my career as I intend, I simply haven't time to waste on algebra and geometry and science and all the other stuff you seem to learn at school. I ought to be doing six hours' practice a day. And there's all the theoretical side of it as well—harmony, counterpoint, thoroughbass; and on top of that, sonata and fugue form. I've done next to nothing at those and honestly, Cousin Guy, they are *necessary!*"

"But bless me, what's to become of your education if you spend all your time on that sort of thing?" he demanded irritably. "No, no, Nina! A couple of hours a day at the piano—or even three, perhaps, if you want extra. But seventeen or eighteen is quite soon enough to begin to specialize like that."

"You don't understand!" she retorted. "I want to be a concert pianist—and I don't want to mess about at it.

I mean to be in the first rank if I possibly can. That means starting young—almost as young as the great ballet dancers have to start. My father," her lips quivered and she had to stop to steady her voice, "understood. I used to give three hours a day to lessons; but the rest of the time I gave to my music. Oh, don't you *see?*"

To be strictly truthful, Sir Guy did *not* see. To his way of thinking, an education of this kind was ill-balanced in the extreme. He had not seen his cousin Alan for nearly fifteen years, since the latter had been seized with an incurable restlessness after the death, when Nina was a baby of eighteen months, of the wife he had adored.

He had gone off, taking the child with him, and from then on they had wandered over a good part of the inhabited globe, rarely pausing longer than a year anywhere. As a result the girl was meeting a relative for the first time and she did not like the experience overmuch. Sir Guy was given to plain speaking and he had let her see that he was horrified at the way her lessons had been treated.

He spoke now. "I wish to goodness my wife had been able to come with me and was here to talk sense to you! Look here, Nina, your father left me your guardian and that means that I've got to do the best I can for you——"

"And that means letting me go ahead with my training," she broke in. "Dad saw that it was necessary. It was what he had wanted for himself, but my grandfather wouldn't hear of it and pushed him into the business. When he met my mother and they fell in love, Grandpapa was furious and tried to put a stop to it just because she was a concert singer. Well, he didn't succeed. Dad went off with Mammina and if he hadn't had that accident to his hand, even then he might have made something of his playing. But you can't do much when you've lost three fingers on your right hand. That was why he turned to composition and he made good there. You needn't think you'll have to pay for me. Dad told me years ago that there was enough money to keep me, whatever happened. He always intended that I should have what he had missed and he's given it to me!" She stopped to swallow hard. Then she went on, "You can say what you like. His plans aren't going to be upset!"

Sir Guy was silent from sheer amazement. He had come post-haste to the little village on the shores of Lake Maggiore where his cousin had been living with his daughter when the news came that Alan Rutherford had been drowned, in the lake, trying to save the life of a child who had tumbled in. He had arrived too late for the funeral, for Mr. Rutherford had held no communication with his family after the death of his wife and it had meant going through his papers to find someone who could come and take charge of Nina. Sir Guy had arrived only two days ago to find that the young cousin to whom he was guardian and trustee had very clear-cut ideas about her own future, and refused to entertain any suggestion about the good school where his own three girls were and to which he proposed to send her after Christmas.

He looked helplessly at the girl. She struck him as needing care. The white wedge of a face under the heavy black hair tumbling about the broad brow looked too small for the enormous dark eyes that were glaring defiance at him. She was thin to the point of lankiness and the beautiful, long-fingered hands with their square-tipped fingers showed every bone.

Meanwhile Nina, having made what she considered

9

to be the full statement of the case, was silent, too. Music was her life. From her earliest days it had been her greatest joy. Even when she was a baby, her mother could hush her crying by playing to her. At three, she had picked out little tunes for herself on the piano and at four, her father had started her himself. At first, he had refrained from saying much about her undoubted gift. He had seen too much of child wonders who flowered early and then vanished from sight. But he *had* seen to it that she practised regularly and had the finest teachers he could manage.

As the years passed and it grew more and more clear what her future must be, he had seen to it that she knew about the hardships and disappointments she must meet if she went in for concert work. Nina had early understood that she must work hard and that there would never come a time when she might rest on her oars unless she meant to give it up for good. She also realized that it was a hard life from other points of view, with perpetual travelling in weather of all kinds, requiring great powers of self-control so that no matter how unhappy or poorly she felt she should not disappoint her audiences. All the same, it was the life she wanted. She had willingly spent hours on exercises, scales and arpeggii that she might gain the technique which would enable her to interpret the works of the great masters. Already, she was brilliant, with a mastery of her instrument that was amazing in a schoolgirl. Her passionate love of her art gave her an insight that had brought from one of her most recent masters the remark that when life and experience had given her the understanding, she might reach the first rank of pianists.

At the same time, she had missed a great deal that is commonplace to the average girl. She had never known the fun of school-life, nor the joy of playing for one's side. She had never had a great friend, other than her father. Games were a sealed book to her, apart from tennis which her father had taught her.

One thing she had been saved. He had always flatly refused to allow anyone to exploit her gifts. He had seen too much of what can happen and, though she was far too old and serious for her age, Nina was free from any self-consciousness or conceit over her music.

Her cousin dimly felt this. He realized that the girl spoke from deepest conviction and, to be quite frank, he had not the faintest idea how to deal with her.

"Well," he said finally, "we can't settle anything now. The first thing to do is to take you to England. How soon can you be packed up?"

Nina started and looked round with a hunted look. "Go to England? But—my father said we should stay here till after Easter."

"Yes," Sir Guy said as gently as he could. "But things are changed now. *I* can't stay here—I have a job of work of my own and I must get back by the end of the week and I can't leave you here alone."

"Why not? Signora Pecci would look after me and I should have my work."

"*No*—and I mean it," he added. "Sorry, Nina, but it's England for you."

He had the wisdom to say no more about school. Besides, he was sorry for the girl who looked at him with such woe-begone eyes.

"But I don't see how I can possibly be ready to go so soon. And how on earth are we to manage about my piano?"

"No need to worry about that. We have a very good one at home—and there's the cottage piano in the schoolroom as well that will do for you to practise on."

Nina drew herself up. "But this is my own—my very own. Dad gave it to me last Christmas when Herr Braun said it was time I had a good one of my own for practice. I can't leave that behind."

Sir Guy whistled. "I didn't understand. And I don't know where you'll put it, even if we can manage to cart it half across Europe and up north to Northumberland."

"I'm not leaving it behind," Nina said decidedly. "It's mine—Dad's Christmas gift——" She suddenly stopped, swallowed, and then rushed out of the room, leaving him to rub his head and wish again that his wife had come with him.

"Alan must have been out of his mind to bring the girl up like this!" he ruminated as he went over to look at the piano. "A Bechstein! And for a schoolgirl to practise on! I don't know what Yvonne will say about it. Oh, lord! What a mess it all is!"

In the end, he had to give in. Nina flatly refused to move without the piano and, in fact, it was five days later than he had settled that they did manage to leave and set out on their journey for England.

One thing happened before then. He came in from a stroll by the lakeside one morning when Nina was playing for her own pleasure and was amazed to find how she could play. His own three all learned, though Anthea had been promoted to a violin at her own request. Alix, the eldest, was considered to be good; but beside the fire and brilliance Nina put into a Brahms capriccio, she sank to the level of a junior schoolgirl. As for Alison, she would come nowhere, and he said so frankly.

"I begin to see what you mean," he said slowly as he came to stand beside the piano. Nina looked up at him, her eyes alight and her cheeks glowing.

12

"But you see, Cousin Guy," she said simply, "it is part of me as much as my breathing is. I couldn't live without it. I suppose for my cousins it is just another lesson they learn at school."

Sir Guy sat down. "Play me something else, Nina. The men are coming tomorrow to box the piano, so it's your last chance for a few days."

She turned back to the keyboard. "I don't know what you like. Beethoven—Bach—Scriabin—what would you prefer?"

"Whatever you please."

She played the first movement of the Moonlight sonata and followed it up with a Bach toccata and Débussy's "La Cathédrale Engloutie." He was more and more amazed for this was no schoolgirl playing but something of a far higher order. Under her fingers, the piano sang the lovely legato of the Moonlight and the Toccata called for an execution that even he could see was out of the common. Of the Débussy, he made very little, since he was not educated, musically, to such music; but he recognized the sweep and thunder of the sea through it.

"Oh, lord!" he ejaculated mentally. "What on earth are Yvonne and I to do with such a girl?"

Then she suddenly lapsed into a minuet, slight, but very dainty and fresh. When she had finished, she turned to look at him again and he saw that her eyes were full of tears.

"That was Dad's," she said with difficulty. She got up and closed the lid down. "I shan't play again until it is in England. I wanted that to be the last I played, here in Italy where we have been so happy."

"Thanks a lot," he replied; and said no more.

But he had plenty to say next day when she appeared at breakfast in a black frock. Signora Pecci had helped

13

her to get it and it was the deep mourning of the Latin races. It would have been trying for even his own Alison with her fair, rosy colouring. For Nina it was simply dreadful, turning her pallor to a sallowness that made her look even plainer than usual.

"Oh, my dear girl!" he protested. "Why *have* you got yourself up like this? Where's that grey thing you've been wearing? For goodness' sake go and change after breakfast. You look a complete sight in that and it isn't necessary. People in England don't go in for such mourning these days."

Nina's eyes flashed. "And let everyone think I don't care!" she exclaimed. "I should have had it much sooner, but Signorina Cavaletti was taken ill and was only able to finish it last night."

She stuck to it and completed it by appearing for the journey in a black beret and coat which put the finishing touches to the awfulness of the get-up. He had to yield. Nina was as obstinate as a mule when she chose and he could only be thankful that she had spared him the long black veil she informed him she should have worn.

"Only I thought it would be so horribly crushed after all those days of train travel," she added.

Sir Guy said no more, and they set off for Basle where they were to join the Wien-Paris express in the evening. Nina had insisted on bringing everything with her and the array of trunks and cases made his heart sink into his shoes. He was going to have a bad time with the Customs. And what his wife would say about it all, he shuddered to think!

Chapter II

ADVENTURE ON THE TRAIN

"HELLO! Here's Berne!" said Sir Guy. He pronounced it "Burn" with a good British accent and Nina was roused to wonder for a moment what he meant.

"Do we change here?" she asked anxiously, looking round in apprehension at the cases and boxes piled up between them, under the seat and on the rack.

"No, no!" he replied. "Change at Basle. Don't worry, Nina. Why, bless me! There's a school waiting here!" as the train swept into the great station and, obviously waiting for it, stood four ranks of girls of all ages from ten to eighteen, all very trim and smart in their long coats and berets of gentian blue. Each had a small case in her right hand and an umbrella and other oddments in her left.

Nina looked at them curiously; but already the train had stopped and, at a word from one of the ladies with them, the blue ranks had turned and were marching in orderly fashion along the platform, up the steps and into the long carriages. It was clear that they were well-drilled for there was little confusion and the girls filled compartment after compartment with the minimum of fuss. Their chatter rose as they settled themselves and Sir Guy broke into a laugh.

"An English school, by all that's good! What's an English school doing over here in the heart of Europe, I wonder?"

He got no further, for the doorway to their

compartment was darkened by the figure of a tall, pretty young woman who exclaimed, "Oh, excuse me, but there has been some mistake and they haven't booked enough seats for our girls. I wonder if you would very much mind if four of them came in here with you?"

"By all means," Sir Guy said with alacrity. "Shove that basket under the seat, Nina and give me that case. Plenty of room," he added to the lady, who smiled and thanked him before she turned and went off.

She was back in a minute or two with four girls, all clearly English, and all much about the same age as Nina.

"Thank you so much," the lady said to Sir Guy as the girls packed themselves in. "Hilary, I put you in charge. Remember, all of you, that we change trains at Basle. Don't forget anything and don't lose either your tickets or your passports."

"I'll look after them, Miss Derwent," the girl she had addressed as Hilary said cheerfully. "Anyway, it's only to Basle. I don't think any of us could lose anything in that short distance."

Miss Derwent laughed and left them and Hilary, having disposed of her belongings, sat down and beamed on her friends. "Well, that's that! For goodness' sake all of you, *glue* yourselves to your tickets and passports. Thank goodness we haven't young Verity to worry about! *She* could lose anything anywhere in less than five minutes if she gave her mind to it."

The other three laughed and a fair, curly-headed person remarked, "It's not really much use settling down in this train. We change so soon."

Then the train started and, as they rolled slowly and majestically out of the station, the girls crowded

16

to the window to wave to another mistress who was left standing on the platform and who waved gaily back at them. Nina could just see her between the heads that bobbed about and was seized with a desire to know more of this school which had such pretty mistresses and where the girls seemed so happy and friendly and on such good terms with everyone.

She was too shy to speak, but she was saved any trouble by Hilary shifting the umbrella she grasped firmly in one hand and digging her foot with it.

"Oh, I'm frightfully sorry!" exclaimed the culprit. "I do hope I didn't hurt you or hit a pet corn or something!"

Nina smiled shyly. "I haven't any corns, thank you, and you didn't hurt me at all."

"That's as well for you," observed a girl who was so enchantingly pretty with her violet eyes and bronzy hair with glints of gold in it, that Nina already felt glad she was in the opposite seat so that she might look at her without being obvious. "Hilary's a hefty wench and she can give you quite a jab with that everlasting brolly of hers! Do put the wretched thing up on the rack, Hilary, and don't be such an ass!"

"Not me!" Hilary eyed the "brolly" with exceeding disfavour, but clutched it firmly all the same. "I'm sticking to it until we've changed trains. Then it can go where it likes till we get to Paris. But if I lose it, Mummy said I must buy the next myself after losing last term's on the boat going home. With Christmas half-way over the horizon, I haven't a sou to waste on things like brollies!"

Nina listened delightedly. Sir Guy gave her a quizzical look from behind his paper. Then he buried himself in it and left her to pursue her acquaintance with the girls. He was quite as much attracted to them

17

as she was and he fully intended that when they changed trains at Basle, he would get hold of Miss Derwent and ask her to let them join himself and Nina in their compartment again.

Until the school had come aboard the train at Berne, Nina had sat silently in her corner, looking the picture of misery, and the soft-hearted Sir Guy had begun to feel almost a criminal for taking her to England against her will. But the influx of jolly girls had roused her and she already looked several degrees happier.

Hilary had been doing some looking on her own account.

"That kid looks awfully down," she thought, calmly ignoring the fact that "that kid" was at least her own age if not older. "Mary-Lou would be safe to do something about her if she was here. I suppose it's up to me to do it. What a ghastly lot of black! I didn't know people ever dressed girls of our age like that, however much they might be in mourning."

Aloud, she said, "Are you going home for the Christmas hols, too? What school do you go to?"

"I don't go to school at all," Nina replied, drawn despite herself to this jolly girl with her mischievous blue eyes and wide smile.

"You don't?" Hilary exclaimed. "Oh, what a pity!"

"A *pity?*" Nina stared.

"Well rather! Think of all the fun you miss!" Hilary said briskly.

"What's your name?" asked the pretty girl. "We can't go on calling you 'you.' It sounds so offish. I'm Vi Lucy and the thing that tried to maim you is Hilary Bennet. These other two are Barbara Chester and Lesley Malcolm. Barbara's my cousin, by the way, and we both live in Guernsey."

"Nina Rutherford," Nina replied, giving her name

18

the proper Italian pronunciation so that Lesley promptly asked, "Do you spell it with an E or an I?"

"N—I—N—A," the name's owner explained.

"Oh, Lesley, you gump, have you forgotten Nina Williams?" Hilary exclaimed.

"Not exactly. But we were Third Form in those days and she was a pree and we didn't have an awful lot to do with her," Lesley returned, unperturbed. "*Why* don't you go to school, Nina? You miss an awful lot, as Hilary said."

"Because I'm going to be a concert pianist and I haven't time," Nina explained.

"Oh, but that's rot," Vi told her severely. "Everyone has time for school—or ought to. As for being a concert pianist, well, we've had Margia Stevens at the Chalet School in the Dark Ages and I suppose you'd call *her* a concert pianist?"

Nina looked startled. "I've heard her play—several times. She's marvellous! Do you really mean she was at school with you?"

"Oh, not us," a chorus told her, Hilary adding, "Vi *said* it was in the Dark Ages—when the school was in Tirol, as a matter of fact. That's where it began and Margia was one of the first pupils. And Jacynth Hardy the 'cellist *was* in our time and a prefect into the bargain."

Nina gasped. "But—but how did they manage?" she cried. "You've got to put in *hours* of practice if you mean to do anything worth while. How did they do it?"

"Oh, if you're as good as all that you get extra time off for it, of course," Hilary explained. "And they knock off unnecessary things like drawing and science and so on, and you get those times for your extra prac. Rather you than me!" she added feelingly.

Nina looked thoughtful. "Surely yours must be a—a very extraordinary school?" she said when she had digested these facts.

The four ruffled up like young turkey-cocks.

"Oh, no, it isn't!" Barbara contradicted her flatly.

"Except in being an extraordinarily decent school," Vi added. "It's *that* all right and I ought to know—I'm the third of the family to be at it."

"Oh no, you're not!" Hilary said. "Counting all the Chesters and the two Ozannes you're the seventh."

"I meant of our own crowd. The rest are cousins," Vi responded with a grin at Barbara who grinned back.

"Oh, I see." Hilary turned to Nina. "*Squads* of them if you count the three families," she explained. "Besides these two, there were Barbara's sister Beth and Nancy—Nancy's at the finishing branch now and Beth's left, of course—and the Ozanne twins who've also left, and the two kids, Barbara's kid sister Janice, who's further along the train with the babies and Vi's young Kitten who hasn't gone anywhere so far."

"She's going to Carnbach to the other branch the term after next," Vi said. "She'll be eight, then, and she's the last of us, so Mummy wouldn't part with her sooner."

"However many branches have you?" Nina demanded. She was looking, as her cousin thankfully noted, thoroughly interested and bright.

"Well, there's us—the school proper, that is—and the finishing branch which is St. Mildred's House. We're up on the Görnetz Platz above Interlaken. The Carnbach branch is outside of Carnbach which is a little town on the South Wales coast."

"I'll tell you what it is," Lesley said thoughtfully, "you ought to ask your people to let you come to us.

20

Then you'd have school *and* all the time you needed for your music. Why don't you?"

"Yes; why don't you?" Barbara echoed her. She glanced at Sir Guy who seemed to be immersed in his paper but was secretly listening with all his ears.

"It's such a frightful pity you should miss all the fun of school and friends and games and so on," Hilary put in. "Do think it over, Nina!"

Barbara began to speak. "When I was a kid," she said dreamily, "I was ghastly delicate. I never did any lessons—not to *call* lessons—until I was about twelve. I was always at home with Mummy before that. I was dying to go to school with Beth and Nancy and the rest, but they daren't risk it. How I used to howl when the hols were over and they went off and left me at home! Then I got measles and was awfully ill, only when I got better, they found that it was *really* getting better. I got fitter and fitter until at last, a year past September, the doctors all said I could go. And was I glad! I've enjoyed every minute of the time and if you go and lose all the fun I've had, Nina, well—I'll be sorry for you! That's all!"

Nina looked unconvinced but, as a matter of fact, she thought more than she either looked or said. Vi took up the tale as she remained silent.

"You'd never think, to look at her now, that everyone in the family expected Babs—oh, well, Barbara, then, Fussy!—to pass out if a draught so much as looked at her. But we did! And now look at her! That's what school has done for her!"

Nina naturally stared at Barbara who went scarlet and turned on her cousin with, "Really, Vi, you're the utter *edge!*"

"That'll do! Pipe down, you two!" Hilary felt that this had gone far enough. "Change the subject!"

Lesley changed the subject to a certain extent. "We have gorgeous excursions at the Chalet School. This term, we went to Zurich and then on to see the Falls of Rhine. That was marvellous!"

"And the term before," added Vi, who was never easily squashed, "we spent Whit weekend above Lac Léman—that's Lake Geneva," she added kindly.

Nina laughed outright. "I know that, thank you. I've stayed there myself."

"Basle—or very nearly!" exclaimed Lesley who had been looking out of the window. "Make sure you've got everything, folk." She turned to Sir Guy and Nina to add, "Can we help you at all? Anyhow, Vi can hang out of the window and grab a porter. Barbara, you take Vi's things and I'll keep an eye on her case. Go on, Vi!"

As a result of these manœuvres, the change from one train to another was made quite easily. Sir Guy settled his young cousin in a corner of the Paris train, saw to all their belongings and then hunted out Miss Derwent and arranged for the Chalet School quartette to come in with them, pointing out that it would enliven the long night journey for his young cousin. Finally, he presented them each with a box of what he called "goodies."

"Now you're all O.K.," he said. "I'll fetch you at dinner time." With which he departed for a smoke.

Nina had dreaded the journey, for she had been miserable to leave Maggiore and she felt desperately unhappy about her music. However, thanks to the effervescent four, it turned out quite differently and by the time they had reached the Gare de l'Est where the Chalet School dispersed in various directions, many of its members being met by relatives or friends, while the Guernsey bunch went off in charge of Barbara

Chester's eldest sister Beth and the rest were shepherded off by the escort mistresses to seek breakfast before joining the train for Calais, she had made firm friends with all four. They said good-bye with promises to write—"if it's only postcards," Vi added cautiously—and Sir Guy whirled her away to Le Bourget for breakfast and the morning 'plane to London, whence a train from King's Cross carried them north to Newcastle.

It is true that once in the northbound train, she lost most of her animation, but at least the look of intense misery did not return to her face. In fact, part of the journey she spent in wondering whether she should ask her cousin to let her go to the Chalet School if go to school she must. And this, for Nina, was something of a wonder!

Not that she mentioned it to Sir Guy. She still had hopes that when he came to think it over, he would realize that a girl who meant to go in for concert work and was aiming at the first rank at that could hardly be expected to spend time on subjects that, to her way of thinking, would be of little or no use to her.

At Newcastle, they were met by the car from Brettingham Park. The morning which, in Paris, had been bright, had changed as they came north and the drive north-eastwards was made through a thick drizzle so that, even before darkness fell, little could be seen of the country, though Sir Guy assured his young cousin that once they had left the suburbs of the great city it was as beautiful as anything she had ever seen.

Coming from the warmth of north Italy, Nina turned cold and shivery, despite the rugs he wrapped round her, and it is scarcely surprising that Lady Rutherford felt aghast when she saw the white-faced creature her husband nearly carried up the steps to

23

the great door where she stood waiting to welcome them. As for the three Rutherford girls, seventeen-year-old Alix, and Anthea and Alison, the twins of sixteen, they didn't know what to make of her.

After an evening in which they did their best to be friendly while she had lapsed back into unhappy reserve and silence, they met in the twins' bedroom out of which Alix's pretty room opened.

"I'm awfully sorry for Nina," Alix said. "I can see she's awfully miserable, and it's been a ghastly day to come here for the first time of course; but I do hope Father doesn't mean to send her to Cecil's with us next term!"

"You don't hope it more than we do!" Alison retorted, brushing hard at the thick red curls she had inherited from her father. "And another thing I hope is that Mother confiscates that awful black dress and the other black things she's wearing and puts her into something decent! She looks a complete freak as she is!"

"Oh, Mother will see to that all right," Alix said serenely. "She told me before I came up that she must go through Nina's things and persuade her to leave off all that deadly mourning. After all, no one bothers much about it nowadays—and certainly not girls of Nina's age. Anyhow, for pity's sake, twins, be decent to her. Father says she's heartbroken over Cousin Alan's death and she really has no one else but us to look to. Don't rag her, whatever you do! I don't believe she'd understand it at all."

"Probably not," Anthea agreed. "All right, Lal. We'll not tease. I should imagine," she went on thoughtfully, "that if she was roused sparks might fly."

"Exactly! And for everyone's sake, we don't want anything like that at present. Let her get accustomed

24

to us." And Alix, who was a thoughtful girl, nodded at her sisters and said good-night and closed the communicating door.

Meanwhile, Nina, in the pretty room at the end of the corridor which she had been told was hers for the future, tossed off her clothes, said her prayers hurriedly and then huddled under the bedclothes and cried till she could cry no more.

Chapter III

NINA HEARS THE NEWS

"NINA, dear, do you know you've been at that piano for the last two hours?" Lady Rutherford shivered slightly as she spoke and Nina, looking up from the Bach fugue with which she had been wrestling, noticed it.

"Are you cold, Cousin Yvonne? I suppose it *is* cold. I didn't notice it before."

Lady Rutherford looked at her. "My dear girl, you look blue with cold! We must try to arrange something better than this for you. At present, come along to the morning-room. There's a good fire there and Alix has made cocoa. A hot drink will do you all the good in the world. Come along! Two hours at a time should be quite enough for anyone!" She shivered again and Nina reluctantly got up off the music-stool, closed her music, shut down the piano lids and followed her out of the room and along the winding passages to the little sitting-room which the Rutherfords mainly used.

A glorious log fire was burning in the grate and, as she came near it, Nina realized for the first time how cold she really was. Her piano had arrived at Brettingham Park the day before and had been put into another small sitting-room together with an oilstove. The fuel shortage made it difficult to give her a fire and Lady Rutherford had hoped that this would be enough for the present. But the day had broken with a heavy January fog which seemed to seep through every crevice and chill the air everywhere.

Clearly some other arrangement must be made. However, the first thing now was to see that she warmed up properly, and her cousin put her into a chair by the fire and insisted on her drinking the big cup of boiling hot cocoa Alix brought her.

"I can't think how you can bear to do it, Nina," Alison said as she sipped her own cupful. "Two solid hours on end!! Aren't you frozen to death?"

"I never noticed it," Nina said simply.

Alison stared and her twin said with a giggle, "Well, I'm glad *I* don't have to work like that! I should die of inanition in a week!"

"It doesn't mean to you what it means to me," Nina replied shortly.

"Well, at least you aren't going to starve any more," Lady Rutherford told her. "I'll see what we can do by tomorrow. In the meantime, Nina, no more practice today, please. We don't want you to celebrate coming to England by an attack of pneumonia! We must think of something to do this afternoon."

Nina's face lengthened and she set down her half-empty cup. "Oh, Cousin Yvonne, I *must* practise! I'm getting all behind! Please don't stop me! I—I'll put on an extra woolly this afternoon and then I'll be warm enough."

Lady Rutherford shook her head. "Not nearly warm enough! Drink up your cocoa while it's hot, dear. It'll do you more good than if it's lukewarm. Give her some more sugar, Anthea. Yes, dear; I mean it!"

Nina had already learned that when her Cousin Yvonne spoke in that tone, she meant to be obeyed. She helped herself to the sugar and drained her cup, but she looked very woebegone. It seemed to her that no one here either knew or cared how she felt about her music. The chances are that she would have disobeyed Lady Rutherford, but when she went back, she found the door locked and the key gone. Nor could she get in at the window. That was latched and, in any case, it would have meant a climb. The house stood on a slope, the ground falling away to the back, and the room where her beloved Bechstein stood, was at the side and towards the back.

As she realized this, anger grew in Nina. She felt that she must, she simply *must* be at work. She ran along to the drawing-room where the fifty-year-old Broadwood which had been one of the wedding presents of Sir Guy's mother stood. But that room was even colder than the other and Lady Rutherford had foreseen that this might happen and locked that door, too. There was nothing left but the schoolroom and what Nina thought of the piano there would hardly bear repeating. It had withstood the thumping of the three Rutherford girls through the last seven years and more and though it was kept tuned, it was tinny in tone and one or two of the notes were inclined to stick. Still, at this pitch, she felt that it would be better than nothing.

Alas for Nina! When she reached the schoolroom, it was to find her younger cousins already there, playing Canasta. They had invited her to join them, but she had refused with a curtness that set their backs up and now they looked up at her entrance with most unwelcome glances. As Anthea had said, if she felt as scornful as all that about cards, she needn't bother and neither need they.

"Did you want anything, Nina?" Alix asked politely.

"Yes; I want to practise," Nina returned, flinging the words at her.

"But Mother said you weren't to until tomorrow," Alison exclaimed.

To judge from Nina's expression, that mattered less than nothing. "You none of you *understand!*" she cried. "I've done only two hours today and I must put in at least four! How can I get on if I don't?"

"*One* day won't make all that difference," Alix told her. "You play marvellously now, anyhow. It won't hurt you to miss half your practice for once. Come along and join us and we'll teach you Canasta."

"I can't play cards," Nina responded briefly.

"We'll show you. Shove up, Anthea, and make room." Alix swept the cards already dealt into a pile and began to shuffle them together. "Come along, Nina. It's good fun and I know you'll enjoy it once you begin."

But Nina was not card-minded. Her whole soul was filled with an overwhelming longing to feel the cold smoothness of the ivory keys under her finger-tips, and she was beginning to feel frantic because this longing was denied.

"Oh, you don't *understand!*" she gasped. Then she swung round and fled for her own room where she flung herself on the bed and cried stormily.

In the schoolroom, the three she had left eyed each other uncertainly for a moment. Then Alison spoke impatiently.

"It's no earthly use bothering. Deal the cards again, Alix. I suppose we must wash out what we'd gained and start over again. But I wish Father had never brought Nina back with him. Talk of a wild-cat! She looked as if she would fly at us the next moment!"

Alix began to deal, but she did it slowly. "I don't like it," she said as she added the cards left over to the pack in the middle. "Nina looks awfully wretched and it *is* a beastly day. Father said she was frightfully upset about Cousin Alan and—oh, let's find her and see if we can think of something she *would* like to do."

"She'll have gone to her own room to howl, I expect," Anthea replied sapiently. "Leave her alone, Alix. She'll hate it if you go barging in on her like that—I should myself, I know. Anyhow, Mother *said* she would try to arrange for that room to be better heated tomorrow. She'll just have to wait for it. But if being a musical genius means being as unbalanced as all that over it, then I'm thankful I'm not one! Your turn to begin, Alix."

Alix was overruled, so no one went to Nina and she cried till she could cry no more and was shivering again, for though Sir Guy had had central heating put into the principal rooms and the hall before his marriage, there was none in the smaller bedrooms where the girls and the two boys who were the eldest of the family slept. Roger and Francis were both away from home at present, Roger with the Air Force and Francis in the Navy, and Nina had only seen their photographs.

By the time four o'clock brought teatime, the young stranger was shaking with cold and misery and when Anthea, sent by her mother to call her cousin to tea, tapped at the door and came in, she was sufficiently alarmed to go flying back to the cosy morning-room to announce that Nina seemed to be ill.

"How do you mean?" Lady Rutherford asked, getting to her feet.

"Oh, she's all shivery and her teeth are chattering and she looks simply ghastly," Anthea said vaguely.

"Where is she?"

"In her bedroom, lying on the bed."

"On—not *in?*" Lady Rutherford waited for no

more, but went swiftly through the corridor and up the stairs to the pretty bedroom where she found Nina as Anthea had described her.

Her first action was to switch on the little electric heater. Her next to hurry to the bathroom where she turned on a hot bath before she came back and made Nina undress and go and soak until she was warm again. By the time the girl had returned to her bedroom, it was comfortable and a couple of hot bottles were in the bed with her nightdress wrapped round one of them. Lady Rutherford saw her into it and tucked her in before she departed to bring up hot tea and buttered toast, telling Alix to attend to her father and the other two until she could come back.

By the time Nina had choked down the tea, she was warming up, but she could not touch the toast and her Cousin Yvonne did not try to force her. She set the cup aside, tucked the girl up once more with kindly words, and left her. A couple of dispirins in the tea would quiet her and relieve the headache which was the result of her passionate crying.

"And now," Lady Rutherford said when she finally sat down to her own tea, "I want to know what started all this? Alix, you tell please."

"I think it was partly she wanted to practise and couldn't," Alix said thoughtfully. "We were playing Canasta in the schoolroom and she came there and we asked her to play but she wouldn't."

"Then she said we didn't understand," the younger twin put in, "and simply *hurtled* out of the room. Alix wanted to go after her but we said it wasn't any use."

"You speak for yourself, John! You never said a word from first to last," Anthea rebuked her. "It was me that said she was probably howling her head off and she'd hate it if Alix went and dug her out as she

31

wanted to. Mother," she turned to her mother, "can't you fix up some way to hot that room enough to let her practise? It's the only thing she seems to want to do and it's ghastly having her hanging about looking miserable or furious all the time."

Lady Rutherford eyed her prettiest daughter thoughtfully. "How much is this for Nina, Anthea, and how much for your own comfort?"

"Six and two threes," Anthea acknowledged, unashamed. "Honestly, Mother, it's spoiling the hols for us. I'm sorry enough for her because she's lost her father, but she really does seem crackers at times."

"I like music," Alix put in, "but I'm not as crazy on it as all that."

"You're not a genius, my good child," Sir Guy said, stirring his tea.

Alix plays jolly well—everyone says so," Anthea said resentfully. "Miss Carins thinks her the pick of the lot at school. I don't see that Nina is so awfully much better."

"Oh, that's rot!" said Alix herself. "I can't touch her at music. I haven't anything like the—the execution she has. And I can't play so that it makes you all weepified as she did the other night in the drawing-room when she played that elegy thing. If Nina joins us at Cecil's, I'm quite prepared for Miss Carins falling all over her and forgetting all about me."

"Yes—is she coming to Cecil's?" Alison asked her father.

He shook his head. "She is not. I don't think she'd fit in and be happy there——"

"Oh, but that's rubbish!" Anthea exclaimed. "It's a smashing school and all of us have been frightfully happy there. Why on earth shouldn't Nina?"

"Well, for one thing, she wouldn't get all the music

32

she wants. Reverend Mother is excellent, but I met her in Newcastle yesterday and had a talk with her and she told me that she made it a rule to allow no girl to give more than two hours a day to music as a good solid education must come before all accomplishments."

"Yes," Alix said thoughtfully. "But then, isn't it *more* than just an accomplishment with Nina? It seems almost as if it were *part* of her—like a hand or an eye."

"Where *is* she going?" Alison demanded.

"You'll hear that as soon as I've told *her*," her father told her. "She ought to hear first. But I'll tell you this much. She's going to a school where they allow for girls who are more than usually talented in any of the arts. They've had two or three near-geniuses before this and they seem to know how to tackle them. I'm sending Nina there and I must say I devoutly hope she'll settle down and be happy. *I* don't know how to handle her; that's certain!"

"Is it anywhere near at hand?" Anthea asked in more subdued tones than usual. Her conscience was accusing her of jealousy and unkindness where her cousin was concerned and she didn't like it.

"Not in this country at all."

"Abroad? In France, then?" Alison exclaimed; but Sir Guy refused to tell them any more and insisted on the subject being dropped.

Nina was kept in bed for the rest of the day and was very glad to be there. When she woke up from the sleep the dispirins had given, she felt weak and tired though her head was better. Her Cousin Yvonne knew that part of the trouble was the shock of her father's death and felt that rest and quietness might do more for her than even her beloved piano. So next day, she kept Nina to her room and forbade the other girls to go near her. She told the girl that she was making arrangements to have the room heated adequately so that she might practise four hours a day when she was released and Nina was satisfied with that. On the Sunday she came back into the family life again and on the Monday, when she went to seek her piano, she found that the fireplace, which had been boarded up, had been opened and a big wood fire, lit before breakfast, made the room cosy and comfortable. Coal and coke were a tremendous difficulty, but there was plenty of old wood in the park and the main difficulty would be for Nina to remember to keep her fire going properly.

"Now," Lady Rutherford said as the girl exclaimed delightedly, "this fire will be lit every day and you may have your four hours' practice on one condition."

"Yes, Cousin Yvonne?" But Nina spoke absently. Her whole being was thrilled with the knowledge that she could practise to her heart's content now.

Lady Rutherford looked at her absorbed face and guessed that she had only half-heard. "Nina!" she said sharply. "Pay attention to me for a minute, please."

Nina woke up and knew that she had been rude. "I beg your pardon," she said. "I didn't mean to be rude. What is it, Cousin Yvonne?"

"It's this. You can practise for four hours every day now, but it must be no more. And you may do it only on the understanding that you remember to keep the fire going as long as we have this bitter weather." She glanced out of the window at the mixture of rain and sleet which a north wind was dashing against the panes.

"I'll try to remember," Nina promised.

"It must be more than that. The first time I find you have let the fire out, I shall lock the room again and

34

what practice you do will have to be on the schoolroom piano. And there's another thing. You must keep this room dusted yourself. Wood fires make a lot of dust and Carson has no time for more work than she already has. I'll give you a set of dusters and you can borrow a brush and dustpan from the housemaid's cupboard. Once a week you may use the Hoover. Now is that thoroughly understood?"

Nina nodded. "Oh, yes. I can clear the grate and light the fire, too, if you like," she added. "I don't want to be a nuisance."

"We'll see about that." Lady Rutherford was inwardly surprised. She knew well enough that even Alix would have kicked at this extra housework for the sake of piano practice; and Alix was considered to be really musical.

"I shouldn't mind in the least," Nina said. "I've often had to light the stove—and clear it when—when I was—with Dad," she added unevenly.

Lady Rutherford stooped—she was a tall woman and Nina was small and slight for her age—and kissed her. "You may do as you like about it, Nina. And child, remember that it is well with your father. He died a hero's death, trying to save a life, so you may be very proud of him. And don't feel alone in the world, Nina. Your home is here—at Brettingham. Perhaps we can't quite understand what music means to you; but we'll do our best to give you music. Now run along to your dear piano and work. I'll send someone to call you for cocoa at half past ten and mind you come at once."

She left the room on that and Nina, dropping her music on a nearby table, went to swing off the baize cover and open the lid before she sat down with a little shiver of sheer joy and began on her exercises.

Anthea tiptoed down the corridor shortly before half past ten, and stood listening as her cousin played a Chopin study with such a rippling of notes as made her own to herself that even though Alix was the star music pupil at St. Cecilia's, she really *couldn't* play like this! She listened for a minute or two. Then the study ended and she went in to find Nina frowning over some fingering. The fire was low by this time and Anthea's first care was to toss some blocks of wood on it before she said, "Come along, Nina! Cocoa! And then Father wants to see you in the study. The fire's all right. I've built it up again for you."

Nina sighed as she rose, but she was too grateful for Cousin Yvonne's kindness to delay. She had her cocoa and then was sent to the study where Sir Guy was sitting at his desk, writing a letter. He looked up as she came in and laid down his pen.

"Come away, Nina! Quite warm? You look a bit different from the misery I brought home three weeks ago! Well, I sent for you to tell you that your school's all fixed up and I hope you'll be happy there and all that. They'll see you get all the practice you want and take you to concerts and so on. The Head assures me of that."

He stopped there and Nina, coming closer, looked up at him with eager dark eyes. "Oh, thank you, Cousin Guy! But please, where am I going?

"Didn't I tell you at first? Bless my soul, I must be wandering! Where are you going? Why, the school I hope you'll like. The school you've met already when we were travelling back—remember? You're going to the Chalet School."

36

Chapter IV

THE FIRST NIGHT AT SCHOOL

"WELL, here we are at last! Thank goodness for that! Oh, *look*, you folk! There's Mary-Lou! Oh, and they must have cut her hair when she was ill. How weird she looks with short hair! Oh, why don't that lot in front buck up and get out? I'm dying to see her and get all the hanes!" And Hilary gave such a mad wriggle, that if Nina, who was sitting next her, had not been holding on to the back of the seat in front, she would have shot out into the aisle.

"Keep calm—keep calm!" Vi Lucy behind remarked sweetly. "Don't have a fit over it! There's the last of them climbing down and off she goes! It's our turn now—Hilary, you ass! Wait your turn! D'you *want* to start the term with a row? Don't let her push, Nina."

Nina, who had been brought to London by Sir Guy and handed over by him to Hilary, Vi, Barbara and Lesley, what time he sought out one of the escort mistresses and explained matters, laughed and clung to her hold while Hilary, recalled to her senses by Vi's warning, sat still, though she turned round to make a horrible face at Vi.

However, they were sitting not far from the front of the coach and in a minute more, she was flying up to the tall fair girl whose head was covered by a short fuzz of hair that looked as if it might curl when it had grown a little longer. Her possessions lay where they were, for in her excitement, she ignored them completely. She was so excited, that the others, still getting out of the coach with due decorum, heard her shriek, "Oh, Mary-Lou! How marvellous to see you again! You look just like your old self—except for your hair! Are you *really* all right now?"

"Just like Hilary!" Vi remarked. "Grab her nightcase, Barbara, and I'll see to her oddments. Nina, you might look after her rug. No sense her getting into a row first go off! Though I expect she'd think it well worth while to have first skim at Mary-Lou," she added, laughing.

Nina had heard all about Mary-Lou Trelawney who seemed to be the leader among her new friends. She had also heard about the Gang to which they all belonged, though Lesley, who was a thoughtful girl, observed that it looked rather as though the Gang would have to break up now since its various members would be in three forms and one of them was a Middle School form which might make it difficult for them to mix as they had done. The other three exclaimed in horror at this, but Lesley stuck to her opinion and even said she had heard Mary-Lou say something of the kind at the end of the previous term when they had been told that she, Lesley, Vi and Hilary were to be moved up to Va next term.

Nina was curious to see this girl of whom they all seemed to think so much. She hurriedly folded up the rug Hilary had tossed aside and followed the others from the coach, but by the time they reached the door, Mary-Lou had vanished.

"Gone in out of the cold," Vi observed. "I expect she'll have to take care for a while yet. You'd expect nothing else after an accident like hers last term. Brr! How bitter it is! Come on, Nina. I'll show you where

38

to go. There'll be no getting sense out of the others until they've seen Mary-Lou and had a good natter with her. She and I are in the same dormy, though, and I can wait. There'll be plenty of time later. This way, Nina. Leave your case, though, and Barbara'll see it put on the truck. Here comes Gaudenz. You'll get our traps upstairs quickly, won't you, Gaudenz?" she added, speaking in German, since Gaudenz declined to speak anything but his own tongue.

He nodded and seized the nightcases which were all the luggage the girls brought with them, all the rest being sent on in advance. Vi touched Nina's arm and then drew her away across the hall where groups were scattered everywhere, all chattering eagerly to each other and the mistresses.

They left the hall and went down a long passage at the end of which Vi tapped at a door. "This is the study," she said. "They moved it last term. I'll leave you with the Head and when she's done with you, she'll send for someone to show you where your dormy is. I'll be around presently."

Anything further she might have had to say had to wait, for a deep, sweet voice called, "Come in!" and Vi opened the door, passed round a screen across it with a muffled exclamation of surprise and then paused to curtsy before she announced, "Good evening, Miss Annersley. I've brought the new girl, Nina Rutherford, to report to you."

"Good evening, Vi," said the musical voice while Nina, overcome with sudden shyness, remained behind the screen. "Shut the door and bring her along. Did you have good holidays?"

"Oh, marvellous! Though we missed Auntie and Uncle and the rest of the Ozannes. The boys flew out to spend Christmas with them, so we didn't even have

Bill with us. Oh, and Auntie Nan had her fifth baby on Christmas Day—a little girl at last. She's to be called Christine Natalie—because of being a Christmas baby, you know—and the boys are thrilled to bits about her.".

Miss Annersley smiled, even as she held out her hand to Nina. She knew Commander and Mrs. Willoughby well, and the four boys whose ages ranged from eleven to four into the bargain. "What a lovely Christmas gift!"

"Isn't it? Auntie Nan said I was to tell you to book her a place here as soon as she is old enough."

"Thank you, Vi. I'll write to her as soon as I get a moment to myself. And now I want to talk to Nina, so you can run along. You know that Mary-Lou is back at school again, don't you? I expect you'd like a short time to discuss this term's changes and see for yourself that she is all in one piece again."

Vi laughed, curtsied and went off, leaving Nina alone with the first Head she had ever met as *her* Head Mistress.

Miss Annersley smiled again at her. "Come and sit down, Nina. I'm very glad to welcome you to school and I hope you'll be very happy with us. I'm sure it won't be the fault of the girls if you are not, nor of the staff. Now to business! Your cousin told me that you would need extra time for your practice so we're going to try you in Va and Vi and the others. I hope you'll find you can manage the work there because it will be easier to give you the time than in the b division. And then, of course, there will be your extra lessons in all the theory."

She had guessed that Nina was feeling anxious about her music. Not for nothing had she had to deal with Margia Stevens and Jacynth Hardy, as well as a number of other girls who were musical if not so highly gifted as those two. She saw that she had been right in dealing with the question at once for the faintly worried expression on the girl's face vanished and her eyes and cheeks glowed as she said, "Oh, thank you so much, Miss Annersley! The girls *said* that in this school you were allowed extra time to make music your career. I do so want to go ahead——"

"I know. You shall have all the practice time you need. Miss Dene will see you tomorrow to discuss your timetable with you. Mr. Denny, our singing master, will take you for all the theory. Do you know any of his compositions—Tristan Denny? Have you heard of him?"

"Is that the Tristan Denny that wrote those three lovely sets of Elizabethan Songs?" Nina asked breathlessly. "Do you mean that *he* will teach me?"

"Yes; he has agreed to take you in harmony, counterpoint and all the rest. Now I'm going to make an appeal to you. In return for all this, I want you to do your honest best with the ordinary lessons you *must* take. Believe me, child, the more you learn apart from your music, the more you will have to give others through it. Your cousin tells me that you speak three languages besides your own, so I think we may cut out some of the work there, as well as most maths and all science and art, too, unless you are keen."

"Not very," Nina replied. "And though I speak and write French and German as easily as English, my Italian isn't so good. We lived a good deal in France and Germany, but we'd only been eight months in Italy when—when——"

"When God called your father to Him? Yes, dear, I know it's very hard on you, but think how much worse it would have been if you hadn't had your cousins.

41

And your father died a hero's death. You must have a talk with Mary-Lou Trelawney some day. Her father, too, died, trying to save life. You may be very proud just as she is. And Nina; I know life seems sad to you now, but it won't be always so. After a time, the pain will go out of your loss and the love and pride will remain to comfort you. And there's another thing. What you have suffered and are suffering now will give more to your music. You will be a finer interpreter of great music *because* of your present pain."

"Oh, Vi and the rest were right when they said you would understand!" Nina cried. "You do! Thank you, Miss Annersley. I'll do my best with other lessons I promise you. And—and—I'll try to—remember what you've said just now when—when things—get—difficult," she added unevenly.

"Good! Then this sorrow won't hurt you, but help you as it ought to do. Now, dear, I have heaps of other people to see, so I'll send for someone to take you to your dormitory. Your cousin, Sir Guy, asked if it would be possible for you to be with the girls you already knew, so we've made one or two changes and put you into Cornflower with Vi and Barbara and the others. Mary-Lou is dormitory prefect. Now let me see." She produced some long typed lists and glanced over them. Then she touched the bell on her desk. "Maeve Bettany came up this morning and is all unpacked. She can see to you. Oh, Miss Dene," as a fair, pretty woman in the thirties came through the curtained doorway at the other side of the room, "would you find someone to send Maeve Bettany to me, please? And when she has found Maeve, ask her to tell someone in VIa that I'm ready for people to report to me now."

"Maeve's in the office now," Miss Dene said with a

smile. "She came to see if she could help, Matron having whisked off her own particular crew to their dormitories. The rest are milling around in the hall, all talking at the tops of their voices."

"Bless them!" Miss Annersley exclaimed. "Well, they'll have to get rid of their steam somehow, I suppose. Tell Maeve to come in, my dear."

Miss Dene nodded and disappeared and Miss Annersley turned back to Nina to describe the winter sports the girls always enjoyed this term. She had only time for a sentence or two when a tap came on the outer door and was followed by the appearance of a girl of Nina's own age or a little younger.

"There you are, Maeve," the Head said. "This is Nina Rutherford who will be in Cornflower. Take her up there and show her what to do and where to go, please. When she is ready, you can take her to Senior Commonroom and leave her there. I expect some of the people she will be with will have turned up by that time."

"Yes, Miss Annersley," Maeve said very properly. She turned to Nina. "Will you come with me, Nina?"

She led the way to the door where she stopped to bob the curtsy that Nina had already marvelled at in Vi. She had had no idea that it could be a part of any English school. Later, she was to find out that when Lady Russell, then Miss Bettany, had started the Chalet School in Tirol, she had incorporated certain of the customs of that lovely land in the school's unwritten laws and this particular one had persisted, even during the years spent in England.

Maeve led Nina along the passage, through another running at right angles to it and up the uncarpeted stairs that ran up from the further end to a broad corridor where several girls of all ages were hurrying about. All of them greeted Maeve, who returned the greetings, even as she piloted the new girl along to a room at the far end.

"Here we are!" she said, opening the door. "This is Cornflower. Come on in and we'll find your cubey."

Nina followed her and found herself in a long, narrow room, brilliantly lighted by four drop-lights from the centre of the ceiling. One side formed an alley and on the other were the cubicles. They were curtained off by curtains of white, cornflower-besprayed cretonne and there was one at the far end with a light directly over it. Maeve nodded towards it.

"That's Mary-Lou's. They've been changing the dormies round during the hols so she gets the end window to herself—lucky blighter! Now let's see which is yours. The names are all pinned on to the curtains." She moved down the aisle and stopped before one midway. "Here we are!" She swept back the screening curtain and Nina followed her and looked round delightedly.

It really was very pretty, for the cretonne was reversible. A curtain of the same was drawn across the half of a window which she knew already she shared with Vi Lucy, having seen that young lady's name pinned to the curtains as they passed. The little bed with its fat plumeau had a counterpane of the rich cornflower blue over it and at the side of the bed was a washable rug with a cornflower design. A kind of table-bureau faced the bed and in the opposite corner was a wicker chair with cushions covered with cretonne matching the curtains.

Maeve went to the bureau and lifted up one end to show that the inside of the lid was a mirror and beneath was a neat cavity for toilet articles. The rest

44

of the bureau was divided into two short drawers and two long ones, one very deep.

"There's a cupboard on the landing where you hang your frocks," she explained. "These are for undies and blouses and hankies and so on. You can use the top for your photos and vases and any books you've brought from home. Oh, and before I forget, you've got to hand your books in to Miss Derwent to be vetted. These shelves below the mirror are for best slippers and bedroom slippers. You hang your dressing-gown on this hook here—awfully handy if you have to get up in a hurry! You keep all outdoor shoes and boots in the splashery—oh, and your beret and coat, too. Your Sunday hat goes in the cupboard *and* your Sunday coat. This other peg here is for your gym tunic. You'll have to wear that for gym and games. You hang your school skirt on it as well. Which form are you in or don't you know yet?"

"Miss Annersley said I was to try Va," Nina replied.

Maeve looked at her with respect. "I say! You *must* be a brain!"

"Oh, it isn't that so much," Nina said honestly. "Music is my chief subject and Miss Annersley says it's easier to arrange for all the extra work in that that I *must* have, than in another form. I shan't be taking a lot of ordinary lessons, you see."

Maeve's eyes danced wickedly. "Then you and I cancel each other out. I love to listen and I like singing, but I'd loathe to go in for it. I want to do P.T.—Physical Training," she added, as Nina looked mystified. "The worst of it is I've got to have Matric if I want to go to a decent college and goodness knows I'm no brain. Bride and the boys got most of the brains that were going in our family. However, I s'pose I'll just have to dig in, worse luck! Got your nightcase?

45

Oh, hasn't Gaudenz brought the trolley up yet? Well, you can't do anything about it, then. I'll lend you my soap if you'll hang on till I get it and then you can wash."

She vanished and Nina removed her beret and coat and settled her cream silk blouse with dainty fingers, by which time her shepherd had returned with soap, towel and comb.

"Here you are! I'm sure you're dying for a wash and brush-up after the journey."

"Well, I am," Nina confessed. "Thank you so much, Maeve. You *are* kind."

Maeve grinned. "Not kind—merely polite. And in this place, we put every farthing of tuppence on good manners, I can assure you!"

Nina looked bewildered, but Maeve gave her no chance to discuss it. "Come on and I'll show you where to wash—though I warn you," she added, "that during the day we wash downstairs in the splashery. No galloping up and downstairs just as we like! Now let's see." She ran to a list pinned to the door. "O.K. You bath in III cubicle 2. Come on!"

She marched Nina off to a cross passage. "Here we are. This is your cubey. You always bath here. In the mornings you can either have your bath cold *or* chill-off. No hot baths except at night. The list will tell you which bath you go for each morning. I mean," as Nina quite frankly gaped at her, "whether you're first, second or third on the list. Go ahead!"

With her head whirling with all the information Maeve was ramming down her throat, Nina washed face and hands and they went back to the dormitory where she unloosened the long thick plait of black hair and combed it out before replaiting it into a

46

shining tail. Maeve, perched precariously on the window-sill, watched her enviously.

"What a gorgeous mop you have! My sister Peggy has long hair, too, but Bride has hers bobbed and—well, you see what mine's like!" She pulled a short curly tress over her shoulder. "Never any longer than that, no matter how hard I brush it."

"But it's a lovely colour," said Nina, who had been admiring the gleaming bronze. "And it's so curly. Mine's as straight as—as—a bar-line."

"You could always have it permed when you grew up," Maeve said. "I like it straight on you, though. It goes with your face, same as Clare Kennedy's." Nina went scarlet at this frank comment. She finished her hair and having returned Maeve's possessions with thanks, waited while that young woman raced back to Wallflower, of which she was one of the ornaments, to put them away. Then she came back and led the new girl off downstairs to a pleasant sitting-room where three or four girls were sitting talking eagerly. Maeve led Nina up to them.

"Hello, folks!" she said. "This is Nina Rutherford. She's to try Va. Felicity, you're there, aren't you? Then will you look after her till Vi and Co. come along. She's a pal of theirs, Barbara told me." She gave Nina a friendly grin and added, "See you later! Best of luck!" before she shot out of the room, slamming the door after her with a good-will that set the ornaments on the shelf that ran round the room above shelves lined with books, rattling.

"*That* will have to stop tomorrow," said Felicity, a pretty brown-eyed girl of nearly sixteen.

"It's only Maeve," observed another, a big, rather clumsily-built girl who was plain, but pleasant-faced. She added to Nina, "I'll introduce us. Felicity is

47

Felicity King and she and Rosemary Lamb—this is Rosemary—are in Va and so am I—I'm Hilda Jukes. And this is Penelope Drury who's in Vb. We five all came back earlier which is why we're here. Pen's been here all the hols—her father lives up here just now—and Felicity and Rosemary have fathers who have jobs in Holland so they can get here earlier than people from England. And Dad had to go to Paris on business, so he said he'd take me with him and give me a couple of days and then shoot me off here the day before if the Head didn't mind."

"But you went to stay at Freudesheim instead," Felicity interrupted. "Lucky you! Sit down, Nina. It's as cheap as standing. Are you really in Va or was Maeve jiggling us? She's a demon and she loves pulling people's legs."

Luckily for Nina, the door opened just then to admit Vi and Barbara and before long the room was full and Nina had been introduced to so many people that she felt bewildered. Mercifully for her, a bell sounded five minutes later and the noise of laughter and chatter ceased with what, to the new girl, was uncanny suddenness. She had yet to learn that while rules at the Chalet School were comparatively few, they were obeyed implicitly as a rule. The girls lined up at the door, Vi pulling Nina into place in front of her. A second bell sent them marching from the room and along the corridors to a very long room where tables, laid with gay cloths, coloured glasses and napkins to match the cloths ran in three rows of three tables each, while a tenth stood across them at the top of the room. Pretty peasant chairs were set at each place and Vi pushed Nina to one between herself and Mary-Lou, who gave the new girl a broad grin as she took her place.

48

There was a silence, followed by the arrival of the staff to the top table. Miss Annersley, sitting in the middle, bowed her head and spoke a brief Latin Grace and they all sat down to bowls of thick vegetable soup, very savoury and smoking hot. The baskets of rolls and twists were handed round and the girls fell to with appetite. They were hungry after the long journey and all their excitement.

Only Nina regarded her portion with dismay. She had a small appetite at the best of times and the prefects at the head of the tables served generously. When the soup was followed by risotto, the new girl's face caught Mary-Lou's attention. She had been talking eagerly to everyone. Now she turned and touched Nina gently.

"What's wrong?" she asked. "Don't you like it?"

"Oh, yes," Nina said. "But I'm so very sorry, I really can't eat all this. The soup was so—so——"

"So very filling," Mary-Lou finished for her with a friendly grin. "I know. Don't look so floored. Eat what you can and leave the rest. I'll speak to Katherine in a moment. Anyhow, it'll be only stewed fruit or something like that to follow."

Nina looked her gratitude as she took up her fork. But it really was too much for her. She was finished long before the others. Mary-Lou accounted for her own share and then calmly rose and went to the head of the table where she had a word with the prefect who laughed and nodded. As a result, when the bottled gooseberries and custard were served, Nina was able to clear the small portion that reached her.

Supper, or Abendessen as they called it here, was followed by Prayers, when Nina had to part from her friends. Vi put her in charge of Clare Kennedy, a girl of misleadingly nunlike appearance, and when Miss o'Ryan had finished Prayers for the Catholic girls, she marched them all back to Hall where Miss Annersley told them that she had nothing to say tonight. Many of them were very tired and they would all go to bed in a few minutes.

"That is, all but the prefects," she added with a smile at those stately young women. "They have another half-hour. I hope you'll all sleep well and wake up fresh and ready for unpacking after Frühstück. That is all, girls. Stand! Goodnight, everyone. Sleep well! Thank you, Miss Lawrence."

Miss Lawrence at the piano struck up a march and the school marched out to bed.

Nina was so muddled with all the new impressions she had received, that she was thankful to undress, say her prayers and snuggle down under her plumeau from which Vi had helped her to remove and fold the blue counterpane. She was asleep almost at once and she never stirred until the clanging of the bell woke her at half past seven next morning to a realization that Cousin Guy had got his way after all and she was at school and felt she was going to enjoy it.

Chapter V

SETTLING IN

"HELLO, folks! Here we come!" Thus Mary-Lou in her breeziest fashion as she headed the group of girls who had been promoted from Vb at the end of the previous term.

"Heaven help us!" retorted Bess Appleton, the form prefect. "Those five desks left vacant are yours, my loves. We've put Nina at that one so that she can have one of you beside her, seeing your Gang seems to have decided to look after her. 'Sort yourselves!' as the sexton said after the parson had married six couples at once!"

Mary-Lou looked thoughtful. "I don't know so much about the Gang nowadays. It seems to me that we'll have to give up going round in a bunch now that we four have been wished on to you and five are in B and the rest are still Middles in IVa Upper. However, that's something we can discuss at another time."

"I should just think so!" Vi said severely as she dived into the seat beside Nina. "I'll sit here and Mary-Lou can come next to me. Hilary and Lesley, you bag those two end seats. Squattez-vous, everyone!"

"Who told you to arrange it all?" Lesley demanded as she sat down.

"No one," Vi admitted. "But Mdlle. will be landing in a minute and you know what she is if you're not absolutely ready for her." She opened the desk-lid and shot in her books. "That's done! Buck up, you three! Dump your loads!"

As a result, when Mdlle. de Lachennais arrived five minutes later, it was to find her form in a *very* tidy room and all sitting straight and looking abnormally good. They rose at her entrance to chant, "Bon jour, Mdlle.," to which she responded, "Bon jour, mes filles. Asseyez-vous, s'il vous plaît!" After which they all sat down.

Her next remarks were in English. "I will take register first. After Prayers, Matron wishes Bess Appleton and Hilda Jukes to go to her for unpacking. Nina Rut'erford," she flashed a smile at Nina, "you will go to ze office to Miss Dene for your timetable. And now, mes chères, register, if you please!"

She took the register and signed it and sent Bess with the little paper-covered book to the office. When Bess returned, Mdlle. was informing the five girls new to the form that they must take certain of their textbooks to stockroom after the afternoon rest. Others would be given them in exchange. Nina, of course, would have everything to get. However, the stationery monitress would see to her stationery during the course of the morning and someone would help her with the textbooks.

"I will, Mdlle.!" announced at least half-a-dozen voices, whereat Mdlle. beamed.

The next moment, she exploded a bombshell under them. "For the future," she said, speaking in her own language, "I shall speak to you in French always—but *always!*"

The form gasped. This was something entirely new. Not that it held terrors for most of them. By the time they reached Va, most of them could talk, if not freely, at least with a certain degree of fluency. Some of them *were* fluent, notably Vi Lucy, whose mother's early years had been spent in France with her sisters so that all the Lucy—Chester—Ozanne clans grew up trilingual. Mary-Lou, with a gift for languages, had decided a year previously that since they were in Switzerland partly to learn French and German thoroughly, it would be wise, to quote herself, to "hoe in" at them, and was almost as good. Yvonne de Gramont, being French, beamed happily at the announcement. Only Hilda Jukes looked horrified. She had little ear for language and she still found it difficult to construct her sentences to Mdlle.'s satisfaction and was wont to declare that never, as long as she lived, could she get her tongue round the uvular R on which everybody insisted.

"Must we answer you in French, Mdlle.?" she asked anxiously.

"Mais oui, vraiment," Mdlle. said inexorably; and Hilda heaved a deep sigh that nearly blew Felicity, sitting in front of her, out of the seat.

"Ecoutez! La cloche qui sonne!" Jill Ormsby exclaimed as the bell for Prayers rang out.

Mdlle. gave the command and the girls lined up at the door, Vi taking care that Nina, whom she seemed to have adopted completely, got into place with the rest. They marched away to Prayers, parting at the corner round which the Catholics had to go for their own morning offering.

There were three more Catholics in the form, besides Nina, and Clare Kennedy gave her a smile as they entered. Miss o'Ryan took the little service very reverently and Nina enjoyed it. She particularly liked the English hymn with which they began—"Just for today"—and the girls' voices rang out very sweetly in it. Prayers ended, the mistress marched them all to Hall for Miss Annersley's promised talk and when both staff and girls were sitting quietly in their places, the

Head left the chair where she had been chatting quietly to some of the others and came forward to stand before the lectern on the daïs.

"I welcomed you all last night," she began in the beautiful voice that rejoiced Nina's heart every time she heard it. "This morning, I want to tell you about some changes we have made."

There was a little rustle at this and every girl looked intently up at her as she went on: "So far, though you have always been divided for games into your Houses, with the exception of St. Mildred's who are a branch to themselves, you have lived together and have been well mixed as to dormitories and commonrooms and so on. This term, that is ended. I don't know how many of you have realized that you are now in dormitories belonging to your own Houses?" She gave them a smiling look, and nearly everyone shook her head. "Well, it is so. Ste. Thérèse girls are sleeping in Ste. Thérèse; St. Agnes, St. Hild and St. Clare, you are all in your own Houses. Furthermore, instead of you all using the commonrooms in St. Clare, you will use the ones in your Houses. On Saturdays, each House will take it in turn twice a term to entertain the others. The remainder of your Saturday evenings will be spent as usual in Hall—I imagine they must be given up to Hobbies Club and your work for the Sale this term."

There was another murmur and she laughed outright before she went on. "Yes; we must think of our Sale. We made an excellent start out here last year and we don't want to fall short of that this term, so I hope you'll all do your best for it. The prefects are having a meeting tomorrow, so I expect we shall be hearing what form it is to take before long—Monday, perhaps?" She gave Betsy Lucy, the Head Girl, a questioning look, but Betsy only shook her head.

"No one seems to have an idea to bless herself with so far, Miss Annersley."

"Well, you have till tomorrow to find some and I hope you'll manage it!" Miss Annersley said with mock severity. "Now I must go on. The pantomime sponsored by St. Mildred's will take place on the last Saturday in February so I expect rehearsals will be the order of the day. This means that you have a very full programme, especially as we are to be allowed to have a School Certificate Centre here this year and most of the Seniors will be taking either that, Higher, or London Matriculation."

One or two people groaned at this prospect and the staff laughed. However, July was more than six months away, so they calmed down and the Head continued.

"Mr. Denny has sent word that he will be along tomorrow at eleven to take some of the choruses for the pantomime and after Mittagessen, if it is fine, we will go off for a ski-run."

The girls clapped at this and she laughed again. "Yes; I thought that would be the jam for the pill! But this is our winter sports term and we must make the most of the snow and ice. It doesn't, as a rule, last much beyond midway through March. However, in March we are hoping for an expedition somewhere. Several places have been suggested, including Zermatt and the Matterhorn; Lake Annecy and, in quite another direction, St. Moritz. I can't tell you yet which we shall choose, but I'm sure you'll all enjoy whichever is is."

There was a fresh outburst of clapping at this and the Head waited a minute before she held up her hand for silence which, much to Nina's amazement, came with almost stunning suddenness.

Miss Annersley resumed. "I have one alteration for

you there. Hitherto, we have taken our expeditions in a body. This term, we are dividing up—Seniors, Middles and Junior Middles and Juniors. We really are too many to parade about the streets of any town and it will be easier all round."

This statement was met with silence, but one or two of the elder Middles pulled long faces. These were the members of The Gang who had not seen as far as Mary-Lou and had no idea that in future they would be going about in smaller groups, though a special sense of friendship would always remain among them.

Miss Annersley knew all about it, of course. She had foreseen it last term. She had even heard Mary-Lou on the subject while that young woman was in the big Sanatorium at the other end of the Görnetz Platz, recovering from what might have been a tragic accident though, being Mary-Lou, once she found that there was no serious damage, she had set herself to recovering at top speed and had done it far faster than anyone had expected. No one had thought she would be ready for school at the beginning of the term, but she had turned up as usual, her old insouciant self to all appearances, and both Head and staff were thankful to see that she had clearly suffered no lasting harm.

At the moment, the Head contented herself with a few final remarks about the need for keeping such rules as there were and then dismissed them to their formrooms with the reminder that Matron would be sending for them for unpacking and they must go as soon as they were summoned and not keep her waiting. More than a hundred girls take some unpacking and "Matey," as they all affectionately called her, always overlooked it herself so as to make sure that all inventories were correctly fulfilled.

She dismissed them, but Miss Lawrence at the piano,

came forward and said something to her in an undertone. The Head's face filled with dismay which changed to amusement, she then broke into laughter and swung round to the interested school.

"Girls! Just a moment! I nearly forgot to make one of the most important announcements of the lot! As you are now definitely to live in your own Houses, you will want to know who are your matrons. Your House mistresses will be with you of course, but we have had to provide three new matrons who have just arrived. One of them is an Old Girl whom a good many of you will remember—Barbara Henschell. She will take charge of St. Agnes. She is bringing two other people with her, Matron Wood and Matron Bellenger who will go to Ste. Thérèse and St. Hild—in that order. Now that really is all, except that I would like to remind you that while you must be loyal to your House, your entire loyalty must be given to the school. The House is only a part of the whole and while we all want you to be ready to stand up for your own, the school comes first all the time. That is all. Turn!"

Miss Lawrence had sat down at the piano again and at the word, she crashed into one of the *Pomp ana Circumstance* marches and the school marched away to its several formrooms having plenty to think about.

The Va people, mindful of the fact that they were very senior Seniors, went to theirs in silence, though rules about not talking on the stairs or in the corridors were not strictly in force until Monday. But once they were safely in their own room, their tongues were loosed and they commented fully and freely on the Head's speech.

"Well!" Bess Appleton exclaimed as Lesley, the last, shut the door behind her. "What do you think of all that about the Houses?"

"It's just going back more or less to what the school was in Tirol, isn't it?" Mary-Lou said.

"Is it? I wouldn't know. Who told *you*, anyhow?— Oh, but of course you'd get it all from Joey—I mean Mrs. Maynard."

"Right in one! Aunt Joey told me yards during the hols. Verity and I spent Christmas at Freudesheim as Mother and Dad didn't come out here till the New Year. Mother was rocky after the 'flu and couldn't risk travelling until then. So Aunt Joey had us two to spend Christmas and we had a marvellous time. She told us reams about her own schooldays." Mary-Lou stopped and thought a moment. "I wonder! She knew about this, of course. She was probably trying to give us a leg up about it all——"

"Bess Appleton to Hilda Jukes! Matey wants to know if you mean to come and unpack today or tomorrow," said an exasperated voice from the doorway.

The culprits looked up with horror while Katharine Gordon, the Games prefect, stalked into the room looking as exasperated as she sounded. "I wish you people would try to remember messages!" she said tartly. "Now, perhaps, you'll go if you don't want your heads bitten off——"

She stopped there for, so far as the six mentioned were concerned, she was talking to thin air. They had fled without ceremony. To keep Matron waiting when she had sent for you simply wasn't done if you valued your peace of mind.

"Heavens!" cried Mary-Lou, giving up the question of Joey Maynard's schooldays for the time being. "Where's Nina? Come on, Nina! Miss Dene said you were to go to her after Prayers. Come on! I'll go with you and explain that it wasn't *your* fault you're late!"

58

She grabbed Nina by the shoulder and hustled her out of the formroom and along the corridor to the office. "What're you going to do that you have a special time-table?" she found time and breath to ask as they reached the last winding passage.

"Music," Nina panted. Mary-Lou had raced her along and she only hoped that young woman intended to wait for her, for she would never find her way back to the formroom.

"Oh, I see. You must be jolly good. Here we are. Tap on the door and you don't have to curtsy to her—we only do it to the Head. I'll hang about here until you come out." And Mary-Lou made for the window-seat at the end and curled herself up comfortably while Nina nervously gave the door a fumbling rap.

"Come in!" said an abstracted voice; and Nina entered to find the pretty secretary rapidly opening envelopes, stripping them of their contents and examining those before she dropped them into one or other of the two flat baskets that stood in front of her. She looked up with a smile.

"Please," Nina said, "I've come for my timetable."

"Oh, yes. Pull up that chair and sit down. I'll be finished with this in a minute." And Miss Dene went on with her letters, working at a speed that amazed Nina, who had never seen a secretary at work before.

She was as good as her word. The new girl had just sat down when she picked up the last letter, glanced at its contents and consigned them to the right-hand tray. Then she pushed both to the far side of her big desk, opened a drawer and drew from it a big sheet of paper which she spread in front of her.

"Bring your chair up to mine while I go through this with you," she said. "Here's your timetable. We've had rather a tough time with it, but I think it's settled at last. Now listen carefully. As music is to be your main subject, you will take no science or art or algebra and geometry. Arithmetic, we can't spare. You *must* be able to manage your own money affairs and you can't do that without arithmetic. So that stays in; but as you won't want any of the public exams, it shouldn't worry you unduly. Miss Wilmot understands and she'll see you understand all you do need."

Nina listened with respect. This was indeed taking her intended career seriously. "I rather like arithmetic," she said shyly. "I don't mind about the rest but I know I must be able to manage for myself."

"Good! Then that's all right. Now for languages. Miss Annersley says your guardian told her that you read and write French and German fluently and also Italian."

"I'm not frightfully fluent in Italian yet," Nina said honestly.

"No? Well, never mind. That can come when you're Sixth Form. Literature, history, geography—you should have all those so they've been left in. You'll have two lessons a week in German and French. The others, you'll miss. You'll take all the games and gym that the rest of the form do. You won't go far in any job without good health and those are necessary while you're growing."

Which effectually stopped Nina's protest against this before she could utter it.

"Handicrafts—you may please yourself whether you do those or not. I'd advise you to go to the first lesson or two and see how you like it. Most of the girls are very keen and it's always well to have something of that kind for recreation." She looked up at the girl. "You see, Nina, if things go as we all hope, you will probably have long journeys to take when you won't be able to practise. You couldn't do much of that in a train or a 'plane. No one can read all the time and it's soothing to have one's hands occupied at such times. So go and try it. That's my advice."

"Yes, Miss Dene," Nina said thoughtfully. "I'll do that."

"Good!" Miss Dene said again. "Now for the music. You will get the two hours a day that all advanced pupils get. You'll see your name on the practice timetable in Hall. Only remember; if for any reason you can't have your usual piano, you must ask one of the music mistresses which you *may* have. No taking someone else's place!"

"Oh, no!" Nina said, rather shocked. Apart from her experience at Brettingham, she had never had to consider anyone else over practice and she was yet to experience the irritation it is to find that you can't use your instrument when you wish.

"Then, in these other times when the rest of Va are having ordinary lessons, you will go to Hall and practise wherever you've been put down for it—see?" She rapidly indicated the places on the timetable and Nina nodded.

"Here—and *here*—and *here*, you will have lessons in all the theoretical side with Mr. Denny, our singing master. He's very good and I think you'll like him. Oh, and by the way, you'll go to all singing lessons of course. That's part of your musical training. Then, on Saturday, Herr von Eberhardt comes up to spend the weekend with his wife who's in the San, poor soul. He'll come here at ten and take you from ten to eleven for piano."

"Herr von Eberhardt!" Nina exclaimed, her cheeks flushing with excitement. "Oh—but—is it Herr Ernst von Eberhardt, Miss Dene?"

"Yes. Do you know him?" Miss Dene asked.

"Three years ago I had two terms with him. And I know Frau von Eberhardt, too, for she used to give me coffee and cakes after my lesson," Nina replied. "Is she ill? Oh, I'm so dreadfully sorry! We were in America at the time, and my father and I were so sorry when he told us that they were going back to Germany and so he could give me no more lessons. Am I really to have him? Oh, how—how *wonderful!*"

Miss Dene laughed outright. "I'm very glad you're so keen. Well, that's your timetable. Suppose you take it and go and study it. You must try to get to know it because it's been a hard job giving you four hours a day and we can't manage a minute more, so you must make the most of it."

"Oh, I *shall!*" Nina breathed as she took the sheet Miss Dene had rolled up and handed to her. Then she added, "And thank you very much for all your trouble, Miss Dene. I'm so grateful to you."

"My job," Miss Dene told her brusquely. "Anyhow, you've got it now. If by any chance we *can* put in a half-hour extra at any time, we will—though I warn you it won't always be the piano in Hall which is where you will generally practise. It's away from the schoolrooms, so you won't disturb ordinary classes, and I understand you've been accustomed to a Bechstein."

Nina's face lit up again. She had already noted the beautiful piano on the daïs and to know that she was to use it for her regular practice completed her joy.

"That's marvellous! And if I have to use some other piano for anything extra, it won't matter because I can always use it for scales and exercises."

"Then off you go. I haven't another minute to spare just now."

"Oh, I beg your pardon!" Nina jumped up and put her chair back in its place. "I'll go at once. But oh, you have been kind to me!"

Miss Dene nodded, laughed, and turned to her next job and Nina slid out of the door feeling that, after all, Cousin Guy had been right in sending her to school—so long as it was *here*.

Mary-Lou was waiting for her. "All O.K.?" she asked, with a quick look at the new girl's face. "But I can see it is. Now come on! Matey has probably been shrieking for us and there's no point in getting her goat. *Scram!*"

Chapter VI

PREFECTS IN COMMITTEE

"WELL!" said Betsy Lucy—and she said it
expressively.

"Don't mind us," Blossom Willoughby
rejoined sweetly.

"I haven't the least intention of doing so. Really,
things are at such sixes and sevens this term, that half
the time I don't know whether I'm coming or going!"

"The Head did say at the beginning of the first term
we came up here that things would take a little time to
sort themselves," Carola Johnstone reminded her. "She
said a lot of our first arrangements were experimental
and there would almost certainly be changes. I suppose
it's taken them till now to decide what should be
changed and what not."

"Including the prefect arrangements," Katharine
Gordon chimed in. "You can't grumble, Bets. At St.
Briavel's, we always did have at least twelve prees and
we had more at Plas Gwyn, according to all I've
heard."

"True for you!" Hilary Wilson's dark eyes danced
as she remembered old times. "And of course we were
all in the one building there, Houses or not. Now we're
divided up properly for living, I suppose we really do
need more prees."

"I should imagine it was more than necessary,
remembering what some of the Middles can be like,"
Carola said. "Anyhow, it's only giving us three full
prees and one sub to each House. That's none too
many, Bets!"

"How right you are! But we'd better drop this conversation and get cracking on the real business. Bring up chairs, you three, and let's begin. There's a good deal to settle and we haven't any too much time."

It was Saturday morning and the prefects were having a full-dress prefects' meeting. At Prayers that morning, the Head had announced the appointment of three new sub-prefects and the promotion of Ailsa Thompson, Lalla Winterton and Elinor Pennel to full-blown prefectship. Sybil Russell, eldest daughter of Lady Russell, who, as Madge Bettany, had founded the school in what all the girls called "the Dark Ages," had been appointed a sub-prefect halfway through the previous term. The other three were new to the job. They pulled up chairs and sat down at the foot of the table and Betsy brought the meeting to order by tapping her pen on the pad in front of her.

"Well, everyone," she began, standing up, "I'm glad to see you all once more—and to welcome our new additions. That being that, I now call on Jean Ackroyd to read the Minutes of the last meeting."

She sat down with a puckish grin at Jean who returned it as she rose in her turn. Jean was Second prefect, a tall, brawny Scotswoman, with reddish hair and the peppery temper that goes with such hair and the keen blue eyes under her reddish lashes. For all that, she was a favourite with the girls, for if she was quick-tempered, she possessed an innate sense of justice and would apologize if her temper had led her into any unfairness.

She read the Minutes of the last meeting of the Christmas term in a voice pleasantly tinged with a Scots lilt and sat down, pushing the Minute-Book before Betsy who scrawled her signature to them when the rest had waved their hands in agreement.

"That done!" the Head Girl said as she closed the book and returned it to Jean. "The next thing is to appoint the duties. In view of the changes, I think we shall have to shuffle them round a little. Jean, Katharine, Carola and I are all Head's appointments so we shan't be affected. But with three new people to call on *and* Sybs who might be described as half-new— or would you call it second-hand?" with a grin at Sybil who promptly made a face at her—"we can afford to make a few alterations and additions. For one thing, what do you think of having a second library prefect?"

"I couldn't agree more!" This was the Library prefect, Peggy Adams. "It takes me all my time to keep track of the Junior Library and the Senior has had to look after itself more or less. And what happened at the end of last term?" Her voice grew shrill with indignation. "No fewer than seventeen books were missing when I came to check up! That won't do, you know. I spent the best part of the last day hunting up criminals who hadn't bothered to return the books they were down for, not to speak of the pair of beauties who had never entered their last borrowings at all! A second pree for Library is a jolly good idea!"

"Very well, then," said Betsy, having listened to this diatribe unmoved. "The point is, does any full pree feel like giving up her present job and taking that on? Don't all speak at once!"

"I do!" Hilary Wilson leapt to it promptly. "I'm not exactly sold on Stationery and I'd far rather be on Library. So you can think of my name, Betsy."

"Right you are!" Betsy made a note on her pad. "Anyone else feel she's a heaven-sent librarian?"

"I wouldn't mind taking it on," Sally Winslow replied. "What about putting Sybil in as Art prefect instead of me? If you *could* say that Herr Laubach has

66

a blue-eyed boy in this establishment, it's Sybil Russell."

"Heavens! If you call the way he regards me as being his blue-eyed boy, I'm sorry for the rest of you!" Sybil cried. "I'd rather be excused, Sal, thanks all the same!"

"In any case with the Sale in the offing, I think we'll have to have a second Hobbies prefect. Some of the kids need a lot of help," Betsy pointed out. "That sort of thing is right up Sybil's street. Oh, no, Sal, you must be Art prefect. Herr Laubach likes you as much as he likes any pupil. But I agree with Hilary about the stationery. Shall we vote on that? Hands up everyone who thinks Hilary could take on the Senior Library?— I suppose that's what you want her for, Peggy?"

"Either she likes. We can arrange it between us later," Peggy said amiably. She and Hilary were very good friends.

"Right! It's your affair, after all. Vote, please!"

Every hand but Hilary's was hoisted and she nodded. "Carried unanimously! That's so much settled. And now what about Sybs for second Hobbies pree?"

There was no objection to that, either. Sybil was an expert needlewoman, very artistic, and with skilled fingers. Also, she seemed to be possessed of endless patience where helping the Juniors was concerned. She received a unanimous vote and Freda Lund, who was first Hobbies prefect, moved down one in case there was any chance of a side-chat.

"And now," Katharine Gordon observed, "Miss Burnett told me last night to remind you that we really needed a third Games prefect. I take the tennis and Carola sees to most of the rest, but we want help with coaching the Juniors in both ski-ing and tennis. Some of those kids didn't get nearly enough proper coaching last summer and Miss Burnett can't do it all."

"Will someone propose someone?" Betsy asked, looking round the table.

"I will." Amy Dunne, a roundabout girl with a cosy manner, stood up. "Ladies, I should like to propose Blossom Willoughby for the post."

"I'll second that," added Freda. "Blossom's tennis is awfully good—no; I'm not flattering her. It really is!—and she doesn't mind helping the duds. And now she's begun to think before she does anything, she ought to make an excellent coach."

Blossom reddened to the roots of her fair curls at this handsome tribute, but she said nothing.

"I'll second that," said Ailsa Thompson who was music prefect and had no wish to change.

So that was decided and Betsy turned to Leila Norris and Nan Herbert, the last of the newcomers. "Then that means one of you for Stationery and one for Magazine."

"What, exactly, does Magazine mean?" Nan asked cautiously.

"You collect in all the stories and poems and articles and so on and sort them out and choose which you think most suitable," Betsy replied. "Then you arrange them in order and hand them over to Miss Derwent for vetting. Then you have to see to getting the thing printed—but I rather think Miss Dene helps you there. You'll have to find that out for yourself. I've never had anything to do with Magazine, though Julie was Magazine prefect that last year at St. Briavel's. I *think* that's how it goes though."

"I see. Thanks!" Nan relapsed into silence and Betsy glanced at Leila.

"It lies between you two. What about it, Leila? Feel like taking on Stationery?"

Leila nodded. "I don't mind in the least. Certainly, Nan would be much better at that sort of thing than I would. She *can* write quite decent essays and it's all I can do to keep in Miss Derwent's good books there. Besides, her father's a journalist. She ought to inherit that sort of mind." She gave the blushing Nan a broad grin.

"Daddy edits a scientific magazine," said Nan with dignity. "It isn't at all the same thing—at least, I don't think so."

"No; but I imagine you have to have the same sort of tidy mind for any kind of magazine," Leila retorted, "and that's what *you* have, my girl!"

"Well, what about it?" Betsy asked patiently. "And I'd like to point out that tempus is fugiting like mad and we've still got to do something about the Sale. Hurry up and make up your minds. No one else will worry."

"Oh, I'll take over Stationery," Leila said. "Nan can have *The Chaletian.*"

"What about duties?" Jean asked.

"That has to be arranged between the prefects of each House," Betsy said. She had had a talk with the Head about it the previous evening. "Splashery and ordinary rules duties are all we have to worry about now. There are fifteen of us and three lots of splasheries to attend to. I propose that we divide up into five lots of three each and keep on the job for a week at a time. That would mean that it would come only once in five weeks for anyone."

No one objected, so Betsy said that she would get out the lists as soon as she could—before Monday, anyway—and it was left at that.

The great subject for discussion was the Sale. All the official jobs having been got out of the way, the girls relaxed a little, but Betsy, with one eye on the clock, thumped on the table. "Order, you people! Freda and Sybil, you can natter about Hobbies all you like, once this meeting is over, but there just isn't time for it now! We've got to discuss the Sale."

The meeting came to order in a hurry. Apart from the pantomime, and St. Mildred's was mainly responsible for that, the Easter Sale was always the big event of this term. It was held in aid of the poor children who came to the big Sanatorium at the end of the Görnetz Platz and the girls were accustomed to straining every nerve to make it a huge success.

It always had to be a Fancy Fair. They could have had an ordinary bazaar, but there would have been an immediate outcry from the rest if that had been proposed. Half the fun, to the younger girls at any rate, lay in the dressing-up and making the setting. *Last year, they had revived a much earlier idea and illustrated the *Willow Pattern Legend*. The year before, when they had still been on St. Briavel's, they had used the charming allegory, †*The Crown of Success* by the once popular author, A.L.O.E. There had been others, notably a *Fairy Tales* Sale when Joey Maynard, then Joey Bettany and a sinful Middle, had done her best during the preparations to slay Miss Wilson who was co-Head of the school and now Head of the finishing branch at St. Mildred's. ‡It had been an accident, of course, but as Joey herself had complained more than once, no one ever let her forget it and it had passed into the legends of the Chalet School. Now the girls set their brains to work to consider what they could provide for this year's Sale.

*The Chalet School Does it Again. †Bride Leads the Chalet School. ‡The Chalet School and the Lintons.

"Let's be original if we can," Betsy urged. "Yes; I know it's difficult, but let's have a shot at it all the same. Suggestions, please!"

Naturally this bland request paralysed all original thought and a dead silence followed. It was broken by Freda.

"Could we do a Georgian Sale, do you think?" she asked.

"Where would you get all the dresses and wigs?" Sally wanted to know. "We've only about a dozen all told in Acting Cupboard and who's going to have time to sit down and manufacture any more?"

So that was out. A proposal from Amy Dunne that they should do *Little Women* scenes was vetoed as too much like *The Crown of Success*. Jean's idea of a Scottish Sale held the same objection as the Georgian one. It would be a hard matter to provide kilts and sporrans for everyone and Acting Cupboard held only two such dresses. Nor did Nan Herbert's suggestion that they should do scenes from Jane Austen meet with any greater success.

At length Elinor Pennell, who had been staring thoughtfully at the ceiling, suddenly directed her gaze at Betsy. "I wonder—do you think we could manage an Old English Fair?" she asked with a little diffidence. "We might have a May Queen and a maypole. And we could use all the stage cottages—we might even manage one or two more. The men would make the frames and it's easy enough to get canvas and paint them."

"That's an idea!" Betsy said. "And it would be something quite new."

"And what about having a merry-go-round?" Sybil put in excitedly. "Oh—not a real one, idiots!" as they protested at this. "I meant we might manage to cut

71

horses out of cardboard and fix up a canopy top. Someone could use it as a stall and arrange the goods for sale on the horses."

"Gaudenz and the other men could move that swingboat stand the Juniors have," added Katharine. "And the kids could have a wishing-well for a lucky dip."

Suggestions followed thick and fast and they made so much noise over it that no one heard a light tapping on the door. It opened finally to admit a tall, dark person who wore a great silk shawl flung round her, sweeping in graceful folds to the hem of her skirt. She stood for a moment, watching the excited girls with dancing eyes. Then she chuckled long and loud and they heard and swung round.

"Mrs. Maynard!—Joey!—Auntie Jo!" exclaimed a dozen voices while Sybil sprang up and pulled out her chair with an eager, "Auntie Joey! How lovely to see you so soon! Come on and sit down here! I can use the table."

"Oh, I had to tool along and welcome you all back again," said the newcomer as she sat down, tossing off her shawl which she laid on the table. "Admire my Christmas gift from Madeira! How many of you remember Miss Stewart who used to be our history mistress? What—none of you? But you've all heard of her, I know. *It was she who wished our one and only Emerence on to us, more or less."

"Do you mean Mrs. Mackenzie?" Betsy asked. "Oh, but I *do* remember her faintly. Sybs, *you* ought to. You must have known her in Tirol. †She married the first year the school was in England and went to

*Shocks for the Chalet School. †The Chalet School in Exile.

Singapore with her husband—not that they were there long," she added thoughtfully.

Joey Maynard nodded. "That's her," she said with a charming disregard for the rules of grammar. "Well, the Mackenzies are coming home for a long holiday. They broke the journey at Madeira and are still there so far as I know, and this arrived for me during the hols. Well, what's the meaning of all the barney?"

"We were discussing the Sale," said Betsy with dignity.

Joey laughed. "So that's what you call discussion! It sounded to me a lot more like several free fights— all violent! Have you reached any conclusion?"

"Yes; we're going to have an Old English Fair," the prefects replied in unison.

"An Old English Fair? Who's the genius who thought that one up? You, Elinor? Go up top! I should say you'd certainly run the bell this time! I'd love to see it, but you'll have to do without my inspiriting presence this year, I'm afraid."

"Why on earth?" Betsy cried in dismay.

"Because, my lamb, we're expecting Number Nine to come along early in April. I'll be far too busy by then for even the School Sale. It's a pity, but there it is. I *told* Julie and Co. last year that the Sale ought to be moved to the end of the summer term in future. They should have passed on my words of wisdom to you and then you could have had me with you. You'll have to be satisfied with my blessing this time—oh, and anything I can do for you during the next few weeks. But you certainly won't see me at it. Now that's enough about me. Who's going to do what with the stalls? It'll mean House stalls this year, you know."

"Oh, do you think so?" Sybil asked from her perch on the table beside her aunt.

"Positive sure! Oh, I suppose the Juniors must have the lucky dip as usual. That's become a tradition. But the rest of you should be at your own House Stall. Let's see. How many will that give you? Five, isn't it?"

"Yes, I suppose so," Jean said. "But we haven't got that far yet. We ought to consult with the St. Mildred's people before we arrange it, too."

"Yes; that's so," Joey assented. "Well, have you thought out the entertainments?"

"We'd only got as far as suggesting sets for the stalls," Katharine said.

"We must have a Country Dance display, of course," Peggy said. "We can use the gym for that. And give eats in the dommy sci. rooms."

"That's an idea. It will leave the Speisesaal for something else. And what about a Folk Play? Here's one for you!" She tossed a bundle of manuscript down the table. "I had a sudden inspiration one day during the hols and tossed that off as a result. When I reread it, it struck me that it might just do for the Sale. It shouldn't take more than forty minutes though you could lengthen it by introducing a few more songs and dances if you wanted to. You can include as many people as you like, too, for there are only ten main characters and the rest can be crowd. I should use mainly Morris in it if you're planning to give a Country Dance display."

"That's a smash—er—gorgeous idea!" Carola cried as she looked up from the play which she had promptly grabbed. "I was wondering how we could introduce Morris."

"And I'll tell you what," Hilary interposed. "What about making a skittle alley and running a skittles competition? I'm sure that's Old English enough. Doesn't Shakespeare mention it in one of his plays?"

"I couldn't tell you offhand, but it would certainly fit in," Joey agreed. "And if it's fine, what about having tilting at the ring?"

"Tilting at the ring?" Again it was a chorus.

"Yes, you could do it with bicycles, seeing we don't have horses much in these parts. Oh, I know you people don't bring bicycles with you, but at least a dozen of us residents have them and you could borrow —if you guarantee to make good any damage that might be done to them," she added prudently.

"But how do you do it?" Amy asked.

"Hang rings the size of embroidery hoops by strings from boughs of tree and people try to pass wands through them as they ride past."

"It sounds rather fun," Carola said. "We'd need four or five people to run it, though. Still, I expect St. Mildred's will rally round. *All* of them won't be needed on their stall. And some of us could help out, too."

"If you do it, I'll promise a dozen little prizes for it," Joey said, "and I expect we can scratch up some more amongst us. Hilary Graves would help out; and Phoebe Peters would, too. I'll do some writing round among the folk I know in these parts and get what I can so you can count that one worry off your chests, anyhow."

"And if it's not fine, we could use the gym after the country dancing," Lalla Winterton added.

"It might be fine and the garden still unfit for us," Blossom said suddenly. "If it's a sea of mud as it was last year, no one's going to let us ride bikes all over the lawn. Still, I suppose, as you say, we could use

75

the gym. We could fix up the rings with sticks lashed to the ribstalls."

"So long as they are dangling, I don't see that it matters," Joey said. "How will you manage for dresses, by the way?"

"Not too badly. There's a complete set of Cavalier dresses we could use for the Squire and the doctor and people like that. The rest can either wear smocks and their gym knickers under, or blouses with fichus and long, full skirts and aprons. That would do, wouldn't it?"

"Caps for the girls, of course. And if you *can* manage it, buckled shoes for everyone. Tie up the girls' sleeves with flying ribbons—and you could introduce some Puritans with close-fitting caps and collars to make a little variety."

"And *that's* an idea!" Carola ejaculated.

Ailsa looked up. "We've got a musical genius this term. Did you know, Mrs. Maynard? She's Nina Rutherford. I heard her practising in Hall last night and I was simply stunned! I never heard any other girl play like that. It was marvellous! I felt as if *my* efforts were just a schoolkid's strumming beside *that*."

"Of course I know about Nina Rutherford," Joey said calmly. "And don't be disheartened because she can play like that, Ailsa. Your own music is good. But Nina, unfortunately for herself, has *genius*."

"*Unfortunately*, Aunt Joey?" Sybil asked. "Why that? I should say she was jolly lucky to have such a wonderful gift."

"In one way, so she is. But you always have to pay heavily for a valuable thing and the geniuses of this world pay very heavily for their gifts." Joey thought a moment before she went on. "I wonder if you'll understand me, girls? It's like a lever,

76

propelling you along one straight path and it won't let you side-track—or not for long, at any rate. Sooner or later, you have to come back to it and no one and nothing can ever really come between it and you. That's why so many geniuses make unhappy marriages. They're so absorbed in their art and it means so much to them, that they have very little time for anything else. You see, it's an obsession and obsessed people are never quite—well—*sane*. I don't mean they're mad and need shutting up; but I do mean that they're lopsided. And the ordinary happinesses of life can never be theirs. Now do you understand?"

"I think so," Betsy said hesitatingly. "I never thought of it before, of course. But I can see that being like—well—like Nina, for instance, may mean that you find it hard to live like other people."

"Exactly!" Joey said impressively. "And as we're on the subject, I'd like to warn you people that if Nina says and does things that strike you as utterly selfish, she won't understand how they look to you. You'll have to try and make allowances for her."

"But Jacynth Hardy is a genius and she wasn't like that—or not altogether," Sybil protested.

"Jacynth is very highly gifted, but from what I can gather, Nina is even more so. And all her previous training has helped to deepen her idea that her art must come first and foremost and I doubt if there can be very much done about it now."

The girls were silent. It was something quite new in their experience and they would have to live with it before they could come to much understanding of it. As Joey knew, some of them might never reach that point. She decided that she had said enough for the moment and turned to something else.

77

"I think, on the whole, I'd better provide something for *every* stall. Make up your minds who does which and I'll send my contributions along as soon as possible. And now I must go. By the way, Sybs, give this to Nina. I want her to come to me for the afternoon tomorrow. Tell her I've seen Miss Annersley and it's all right."

"Can't *I* come too?" Sybil asked as she tucked the note into her blazer pocket.

"No, my love, you may not. I want Nina all to myself. You can come over any time you can get leave and well you know it!" Joey threw her shawl over her shoulders, stood up and draped it. "What are you people planning to do this afternoon?"

"Go ski-ing if it keeps fine," Katharine said.

Joey glanced out of the window. "In that case, my pets, you're going to be disappointed. There are some very suspicious clouds drifting around the sky. It wouldn't surprise me if we had a young blizzard shortly. That sky means mischief or my name's not Joey Maynard! I'm going while the going's good! Farewell!"

She waved to them from the doorway and vanished, leaving them all clustered round the window whither they had rushed on hearing her remarks.

"Well," Betsy said as she returned to her seat, "I'm awfully afraid she's right and ski-ing will be definitely *off!* In that case, Freda and Sybil, you'd better go and ask the Head if we can have a session of the Hobbies Club this afternoon. I suppose we must sort this out and then we can go and see Miss Annersley about it. Hello! Is that the bell? Then it can wait a while. I want my elevenses after all this hard labour. Come on, everyone! We'll come back after and finish up.

There'll be no ski-ing. Here come the first snowflakes!"

And the prefects, taking a last look before they descended to the Speisesaal in quest of cocoa or hot milk and biscuits, were forced to agree that Mrs. Maynard had prophesied truly. There would be no expedition that day.

Chapter VII

TROUBLE!

A S it turned out, Nina was unable to accept Joey's invitation for Sunday. What that experienced young woman had described as "a small blizzard," turned out to be a full-grown one which continued the major part of Saturday, all Sunday and all Monday. No one was going to hear of allowing anyone, least of all a schoolgirl, going out in such a storm, not even when it meant just crossing the two gardens. Miss Annersley rang up Mrs. Maynard early on Sunday to tell her so and the would-be hostess fully agreed with her.

"Oh, you're right, of course, Hilda. Tell the kid it's not cancelled—only postponed," she said. "This isn't likely to last more than a day or two and she can come next Sunday instead. Tell her I'll be looking forward to it."

"I'll tell her," the Head agreed. "But I shouldn't care to prophesy about the snow just now. Have you forgotten that this is January? It's mid-winter and *anything* might happen!"

"Don't be so pessimistic," was all she got in return. "It wouldn't *dream* of going on after tomorrow. It's not that kind of blizzard. Besides, I want to have Jo Scott and Mary-Lou and Jessica Wayne and one or two other people before I'll have to give up parties for a few weeks. You give Nina my message."

"I will. Are you all right, Joey?"

"Flourishing like the green baytree—or no; I don't

80

think that's a very *nice* simile, seeing I don't think I'm what old King David meant by 'the wicked.' But we're all very well. I'm having a treat to myself. Jack was at home last night and as he can't possibly get to the San through this, I'll have him to myself all day for once and the other men can run the San on their own. It doesn't happen very often, so I'm making the most of it. Give my love all round. I'm ringing off now."

"One moment, Joey. You'll like to know that we all think the Old English Fair is a stroke of genius. And your idea of tilting at the ring has intrigued everyone hugely."

"Thought it would!" quoth Joey. "I *must* go! It's breakfast time."

"At ten to ten: You're very late!"

"Well, rather! This was a chance for Jack to have a good long sleep after a series of either broken or late nights, so I left him to have his sleep out. Anna gave me some coffee when I showed up so that I wasn't fasting. He roused half-an-hour ago and now I hear Anna bringing things into the Speisesaal so I must go. See you sometime sooner or later!" And Joey rang off with great firmness.

Miss Annersley laughed as she turned away from the telephone. "It's a blessing Anna's there to keep an eye on Jo and her doings! Send Nina to me, will you, Rosalie, and I'll explain to her what's happening."

Miss Dene laughed. "Did you know that Joey means to offer the loan of her piano for Nina to practise on when Hall is otherwise engaged? She told me when she ran in yesterday morning. It's as well the child doesn't know, isn't it? But Joey told me to leave it to her, so I said nothing."

"That's like Joey," the Head said appreciatively. "Run along and fetch her, will you? I said we'd have our home services at half past ten and I want to explain to her before then."

Miss Dene went off and Nina came to the study and listened to the explanation with a gravely polite air.

"I see. Thank you, Miss Annersley. If you are ringing up Mrs. Maynard, will you please tell her I shall be looking forward to next Sunday?"

Miss Annersley agreed and dismissed her, thinking to herself that while politeness was a desirable thing in girls, she preferred something a little less grown-up in teenagers. Then she turned to sort out her books and forgot the matter for the time being.

On Tuesday, the school woke up to find that the storm was over though, even so, there could be no going out for them at present. The newly-fallen snow was too soft and they must wait until either the men had beaten out some paths or the frost firmed it enough for skis. There were deep drifts all round and no one wanted the bother and anxiety of having to dig down into them for buried girls!

Nina, practising happily while the rest of Va attended an algebra lesson with Miss Wilmot, thought that, on the whole, things might have been very much worse. She had already enjoyed a session on *Henry V* with Miss Derwent and another on the effects of the great ocean currents on the climates of various parts of the world with Miss Moore. Now she had an hour at the piano, since algebra for Va was followed by dictée this morning and from that, she was excused. She settled down to a Bach three-part Invention with much enjoyment and worked with a will. Her first lesson with Herr von Eberhardt had been delightful. She had liked him when she had had lessons from him in America and he was rejoiced to have under his teaching again the girl he had felt sure was to make history in the world of music.

Actual trouble first began after Abendessen, as the school called supper. The members of St. Clare, to which House she had been assigned, were in their commonroom. The Juniors and Junior Middles had a playroom next door. Everyone else used the commonroom in free times and that evening, they were all there, reading, knitting, doing embroidery or making jigsaw puzzles. A bunch of the Middles had annexed the big table to one side of the room and were playing a noisy game of rummy. Nina had sat down with the library book Vi Lucy had seen she got on the Saturday, but Nina's fingers were itching for the touch of the cold ivory keys. Everyone else was fully occupied, even Vi sharing a jigsaw with Mary-Lou and Hilary. She looked round, saw that nobody was bothering about her and slipped quietly out of the room and made for Hall.

The place was in darkness, but already she knew where the switches were. She switched on the double lights over the daïs, opened the piano and sat down. A minute later, she was lost to the world as she wrestled with the Bach again. She had not been there more than five minutes, however, when the door opened and Miss Dene came in.

"So it *is* you, Nina?" she said as she mounted on to the daïs. "I thought so! My dear girl, I'm very sorry, but whether you know it or not, you're breaking all sorts of rules by practising now. You've had your four hours today, haven't you?"

"Yes; but there are two passages I simply couldn't get right and I did want to finish them today if I could. Oh, Miss Dene, please let me go on! Just for half-an-hour! I promise to give up after that!"

83

Even as she spoke, her fingers were back on the keys again, touching them lovingly, as Rosalie could see, though she shook her head at the request. "I'm afraid I mustn't, Nina. Rules say that no girl may do any work after the end of prep—and that includes practice, I'm sorry to say. You must stop now."

"But I'm not interfering with anyone and no one will miss me," Nina urged.

"That isn't the point, my lamb. You girls have a full timetable and are expected to work hard at the proper time. But a certain amount of recreation you *must* have, so the end of prep is the end of all work. Believe me, you'll do much better work tomorrow if you take a story book or join in some game or other. Besides," she added, laughing, "if we gave way to you, we should have to give way to someone who wanted to do science, or art or history or gym. It can't be done. Staff need rest as much as you girls. Come along! Put your music away and close up the piano and run along back to the commonroom."

Nina's face fell, but she remembered her promise to Miss Annersley on that first morning, so she did as she was told without any more fuss and went back to the commonroom where Mary-Lou and Vi called to her to come and help them with their jigsaw. She went and found that this pursuit, which was new to her, was an absorbing one, so that she was well occupied for the rest of the evening.

Once she had gone, however, Miss Dene locked the piano and removed the key which she took to Miss Lawrence, the head of the resident music staff.

"You'd better see to that piano being locked every night," she warned that lady. "Judging by what Joey had to say on Saturday morning, if you're a genius, ordinary rules mean less than nothing to you if they happen to run counter to your art."

"Oh, she's quite right there," Miss Lawrence agreed. "All right; I'll see to the piano. And it may be as well to keep the others locked, too. If she really yearns to practise, she'll find somewhere if it's humanly possible."

"So Joey says. All right; I'll leave it to you, Dorothy, and *don't*, I implore you, go and lose any of the keys."

"What do you take me for?" Miss Lawrence said scornfully. "That *would* be a lovely excuse to some of those lazy monkeys to get out of practice!"

It was left at that, but Nina did not discover what was happening for a day or two.

On Wednesday, they found that the frost had struck during the night. The snow was hard as iron and Miss Annersley decreed that after Prayers they were all to wrap up and go out for a ski-run until eleven o'clock. It was winter and the rule of the school had always been that in winter every opportunity must be taken of open-air exercise. During the long snowstorms they had to be penned up so closely, and the doctors from the big Sanatorium were insistent on this. From the very beginning the school had been run in conjunction with the Sanatorium, first when both were at the Tiernsee in Tirol; then with the one opened in the Welsh Hills; now with the new one at the farther end of the Görnetz Platz. Many of the girls were delicate or came from families with a bad medical history and health was set first and foremost all the time.

"Must we wear our coloured glasses?" Betsy asked when the Head had made her announcement.

Miss Annersley shook her head as she glanced out of a nearby window at the grey sky. "No; there's no need," she said. "The radio prophesies a further fall of snow later on and I very much doubt if the sun struggles through *that* ceiling of cloud at all today." She paused. Then she added, "Wrap up well, all of you. It's bitterly cold outside."

"Have you ever ski-ed before?" Hilary Bennet asked Nina as they pulled on their ski-ing suits with the close-fitting hoods that protected their ears and then pulled on warm, woolly mitts.

"Oh, yes, often," Nina replied—it was English day and the English girls were taking every advantage of that fact. "I've always enjoyed it—I think it comes the nearest thing to flying. I'm so glad we do it here."

"We toboggan, too," Vi put in as she picked up her skis. "Only we haven't done much at that since Mary-Lou's accident last term." She shuddered. "That was a ghastly time. She was concussed, you know, and she didn't come to for days and no one could say whether she'd be all right or not."

"Is that why her hair's so short?" Nina asked with interest.

"Yes; Uncle Jack—Dr. Maynard, you know—had it all shaved off. She used to have the loveliest long pigtails—she called them her 'Kenwigses.' Then she went in for one tail. I've heard that when she found she was minus hair of any kind, she blew up good and hearty. Luckily, her hair has always grown quickly, and she doesn't look too bad now. And it's growing in curly, so she's resigned."

"Aren't you folk ready yet?" demanded Mary-Lou herself. "Come on then!"

Nina followed them out of the splashery, along the narrow passage and out into the corridor Gaudenz, one of the men who worked at the school, had dug out early that morning. Then she strapped on a pair of well-worn skis. When she stood up and moved out of the way, it was clear that she was no novice. Her motion as she skimmed over the frozen snow was delightfully easy.

"Good for you!" Hilary remarked as she joined her. "Come on—this way. We meet the crowd in the front drive and then we'll be told which way we're to go."

In the front drive, the sixteen people who made up Va gathered together and were joined by Miss o'Ryan who was an expert on skis, thanks to many years spent in Tirol in her childhood. She told them to follow her and when they were in the road, directed them to turn to the left. "We'll try to get as far as St. Anton," she added. "Let me see. Nina, you can obviously use skis, so we haven't any novices here. We ought to do it easily and be back by eleven for Break. Lead on, Mary-Lou and Hilary. And don't go too far ahead, please."

The pair set off and the rest of the form followed, flying over the snow, looking not unlike a flock of brightly coloured birds in their gentian-blue suits with the crimson trimmings. It was bitterly cold as the Head had said, but the strenuous exercise soon warmed them up and by the time they had reached St. Anton, a tiny village of chalets with a small, white-washed church with the usual bulbous spire, at the far end of the place, even Nina's usually pale cheeks were pink. They skimmed round the church and then set off for home. Their chatter and laughter carried on the crisp air and Nina laughed and talked with the rest. If Sir Guy could have seen her just then, he would have been thankful. He had worried considerably about the miserable appearance of his young cousin.

"It's just as well you ski so well," Vi said as she

and Nina raced along, side by side. "Do you skate, or don't you dare in case of accidents? I suppose one has to be careful about wrists and fingers. It would be rather bad if *you* broke anything, wouldn't it? I mean, how could you practise?"

"I can skate all right," Nina said. "My father taught me when I was just a little thing of six or so. But you're quite right, Vi. I should be frightfully worried if I had any sort of an accident like that."

"Oh, well, if you've done it practically all your life, I don't suppose you need worry about it," Vi said soothingly.

"Can't we hurry?" Nina asked. Vi's remarks had reminded her that time was flying and she did not want to miss any of her practice.

"Not to get ahead of the leaders," Vi replied. "That's never allowed."

Nina sighed. She felt in her bones that at least half her practice time was going to be cut this morning and she didn't like it. However, Mary-Lou and Hilary made good time and they swept round the house to their own door just as the clock was chiming eleven. But even then, as Nina found, there was no just discarding her suit and flying to her beloved piano. She had to go and get her milk and biscuits with the rest and it was quite a quarter past eleven before she was able to sit down and begin work in the Schumann sonata in G minor that Herr von Eberhardt had given her at her lesson on the Saturday morning.

She wasted no time. She set to work at once and Miss Lawrence, happening to pass the upper door of Hall as she crossed over to the study, was attracted by the sounds and opened the door quietly. She was amazed at what she heard. Nina was working with a concentration that the mistress wished her own pupils would use. She let nothing slip. The music mistress noted how she played one stiff passage over and over, first the right hand, then the left, then both together until she had it as she felt it should be. Further, she was listening intently to what she was doing. She stopped and tried two or three different fingerings of one run before she was satisfied that she had the right one.

"That girl should go far," the mistress thought as she closed the door softly and went on her way. "But what a touch—what technique for a child of fifteen— how she can work! I'd like some of my own beauties to hear her! It might open their eyes a little."

Twelve o'clock came all too soon for Nina, but when the bell rang, she had the sense to stop, pack up her music, close the piano, pulling its baize cover over it, and hurry off to her formroom where she was due for a lesson in English.

For the first hour of the afternoon session, she was practising again. After that, Va had games. Ordinary games were out of the question, however, for the snow had come back—much more gently, but still it was falling again—and the girls had to resign themselves to no outdoor exercise until it stopped.

Word came from Miss Burnett that as ski-ing or tobogganing was out of the question, the girls were to change into tunics and plimsolls and come to the gym. This no longer meant going outside, for during the long summer holidays, wooden passageways had been built, linking the art room, domestic science kitchens, geography room, science laboratories and the gym with the school proper. In fine weather, the girls might and did cross over outside; in weather like this, they had to march decorously along the corridors.

Led by Bess as form prefect, Va went quite joyfully,

so far as most of them were concerned. Miss Burnett was waiting for them and with her was Mdlle. Lenoir, the junior music mistress.

"Well," said the P.T. mistress when they were all in the big room, "any sort of outdoor games can be counted out at the moment. Mdlle. Lenoir has twenty minutes to give us, though, so we'll begin with country dancing. Let me see; Nina, have you done any!"

"Only what we did on Saturday night," Nina replied, having been hauled in and dragged through half-a-dozen of the easier dances by Mary-Lou and the rest of that quartette.

"Oh, well, we'll begin with *Butterfly*. That's easy enough. Take your partners, girls. Yes, Hilary; you take Nina and help her through."

Butterfly was followed by *Bonnets So Blue*. Then, with an eye to the needs of the others, Miss Burnett told Nina to sit out and took her place while the girls danced *Parson's Farewell* and *Maid in the Moon*. Then Mdlle. Lenoir had to go to give music lessons and Miss Burnett suggested a round of Beanbags to give them a chance to get their breath. Two of the girls "picked up" for sides and then they all sat on the floor cross-legged in two circles with a good distance between each girl.

For Nina's sake, the mistress explained the game. "Beginning with your leader, you toss the bags from one to another all round the circle. The last girl to receive the bag runs with it to me and collects the next one which she tosses as soon as she has sat down *properly*. That means cross-legged and right down on the floor. There are eight bags for each ring, so everyone will have a turn at bringing the bag and beginning the tossing. The ring who first brings me the last bag wins. Got your bags, Bess and Hilda? Then begin—NOW!"

The fun began. The bags went whirling round the rings and Mary Yates, the last in Nina's ring, was up half a second before Vi Lucy and tearing up the length of the gym to toss the bag to Miss Burnett, grab the second one, come racing back and sit down. However, Vi gained time by crossing her legs and dropping to the ground that way so that the new bags started the round together. By the time it came to Nina's turn, she had grasped what was wanted and she was on her feet and flying down to the mistress before Rosemary King had sprung up. Back came Nina, full tilt, moving Hilary to mutter to Lesley Malcolm who was next to her, "Some sprinter!" She dropped into her place, feet crossed, and the bag went on its journey before Rosemary could sit down. Thanks to this, Hilda's side won by one second and the other ring clapped them vigorously.

"Leapfrog to wind up," Miss Burnett decided. "That ought to shake all the fidgets out of you! Round the room, and mind you space out evenly. Mary-Lou, show Nina what to do. And remember, girls; you only *touch* the back of the girl you are leaping over. Don't press with all your weight. Hilda, be careful! People being leaped over, remember to keep your heads down."

Mary-Lou took over Nina in her usual capable manner. "Stand here," she said. "Stoop down and grip your ankles—or as near them as you can get. No; keep your feet apart a little to get a firm stance. Now, you're the last, so you'll jump last. When we do it in the garden, of course, we start off as soon as we've been jumped but we can't do that here. Grass

91

is soft to fall on and wood isn't. Now do you quite understand?"

Nina said she did and Mary-Lou went off to her own place, while Bess got ready to do the round. The new girl gasped as she saw long-legged Bess leap lightly over girl after girl in her run round the room. Then the form prefect was coming up to her, so she remembered what Miss Burnett had said and tucked her head in. A minute later there was the light touch of hands on her back and Bess was over and running to stand further along, bent down for Mary-Lou to follow her example.

All went well with the first seven and Nina was enjoying the fun. Then Hilda Jukes came. Now Hilda was a big creature, kind, pleasant and very well-meaning, but as heedless a girl as you could find anywhere. Miss Burnett warned her once more about not bearing with her whole weight on the bent backs and started her off. Hilda remembered most of the way round. Then she came to Vi who was behind Nina. In her excitement, she forgot and if Vi had not been prepared, she would have been bowled over. As it was, she just managed to keep her balance. Nina, new to the game, was not prepared at all. Hilda clamped a pair of big hands firmly on her, bore down and leapt. Nina gave way and the pair of them rolled over, Nina undermost.

Miss Burnett rushed to the spot at once and hauled Hilda off with more speed than gentleness. Then she bent over the new girl who was sitting up, holding her left wrist with the other hand and biting her lips to keep from crying out with the pain. Somehow, she had bent the wrist under her and Hilda's weight on top had done the mischief.

The mistress examined the injured wrist gently but

thoroughly, while Hilda, having come to her senses, stood gasping out apologies.

"Shut up, ass!" Mary-Lou said, hushing her. "Shall I get Nina some water, Miss Burnett?"

"Yes—do," Miss Burnett replied. "No, Nina; no bones broken, but you've given that wrist a nasty wrench. You must go to Nurse and she'll bandage it for you and give you a sling to rest it. It'll be all right in a day or two. Thank you, Mary-Lou!" as that young woman brought the water. "Sip this, Nina, and then I'll take you to Nurse. Thank goodness there's no serious harm done!"

No one was prepared for what followed. Nina gave her a look of horror. "But—what about my practice?" she cried.

"I'm afraid it'll have to go for the present. Don't look so upset, Nina," Miss Burnett said soothingly. "A couple of days' rest will probably be all your wrist will need. You ought to be able to get back to your piano by Monday."

"Oh, I'm awfully sorry, Nina!" cried tactless Hilda at this moment.

Nina swung round on her, her eyes flashing. "You clumsy creature!" she exclaimed. "You were warned twice! Now you've stopped my practice! I'll never forgive you—never!" And with the final words, she burst into a passion of tears.

Chapter VIII

MARY-LOU SEEKS ADVICE

"AND so, you see, although Hilda's said over and over again how sorry she is, Nina just won't listen to her. The last time I saw it happen, she turned her back and walked away before Hilda had well begun. I think, myself, she's an idiot— Nina, I mean—for it *was* an accident, even though Hilda should have had more sense than to bear all her weight down on *anyone*, let alone a girl who, to judge by what she says, had never played leapfrog before in her life. I should think," concluded Mary-Lou seriously, "that that's one thing Hilda will never do again."

"Then that's so much to the good—so far as Hilda is concerned," Joey Maynard said ruthlessly. "I'm sorry for her, but she really is a heedless creature and always has been. If she's learnt her lesson through this silly business, it'll be a mercy!"

"Yes, but it's not helping Nina. Everybody's told the silly kid that her wrist will be all right in a few days' time, but the way she's going on about it, you'd think she was maimed for life. Matey sent for Dr. Graves as Uncle Jack wasn't available and he's stopped her practice altogether until Monday and you'd think the world was coming to an end!" Mary-Lou said graphically. "What can we do about it, Auntie Jo?"

Joey finished clipping together the last sheets of the carbon copy of her new book. Then, as she added them to the pile, she said slowly, "But the trouble is that's exactly what she *does* feel."

Mary-Lou gaped at her. "Just because she's wrenched her wrist and is cut off from practice for a few days? She couldn't possibly!"

"Oh, yes, she could. You're forgetting that the be-all and end-all of life for her *is* music." Then, as Mary-Lou still looked completely incredulous, she added, "I can understand to a certain extent for I've had spasms of feeling that way myself when I had a chapter of the current book all boiling up in my brain and haven't been able to get down to it at once. And remember this: with Nina it's genius and that makes it a thousand times worse."

"Then what is it with you?" Mary-Lou demanded. "If anyone asked me, I'd say *you* were a genius—writing, not music," she added.

Joey shook her head. *"No,* thank heaven! I'd be sorry for your Uncle Jack and the family if it were. It's talent where I'm concerned, Mary-Lou, and that's not nearly such an urgent thing as genius."

Mary-Lou turned this over in her mind and then dismissed it until she had leisure to think it out for herself. At present, she was limited to one hour away from school and nearly half of that had gone already. It was the Saturday after the accident and, as she had said, Nina stayed grimly unforgiving where the penitent Hilda was concerned. She either could not or would not see that the whole thing was an accident—one due to sheer carelessness, it is true; but still an accident.

Hilda herself had heard all about her part in the affair, first from Miss Burnett who had been righteously angry because all her warnings had been ignored. She had not spared Hilda a severe tongue-lashing which had reduced the culprit nearly to tears. The Head who came next had pointed out that if she could still be so heedless at her age, she was hardly fit to be in Va with every likelihood of going up to one or other of the Sixths in September and the possibility of being otherwise eligible for a prefectship.

"If you are going to behave so irresponsibly, Hilda, how can we promote you?" Miss Annersley had said gravely. "You are sixteen and a half now—seventeen in May, isn't it? And yet in some ways you are nearly as heedless and careless as little Margot Maynard. How can we dare to rely on you if you aren't going to try to improve?"

When Hilda got herself out of the study, what was left of her might have gone into a half-pint mug!

Her own form, needless to state, told her *their* opinion with brutal frankness. Miss Lawrence had crowned everything that morning when she happened to meet the girl, by telling her exactly what she thought of her for upsetting Nina's music. This had been the finish so far as Hilda was concerned. She had vanished from sight and when Mary-Lou at last found her in the art storeroom where she had hidden herself, she had cried until she was fit for nothing but Matron's care. Being a canny young person, Mary-Lou had refrained from any comments about absence from mending and letter-writing. Instead, she fetched Matron and Matron marched Hilda off to her cubicle and told her to lie down for an hour or two after she had sponged her face.

During Break, Mary-Lou and her three chums had neatly cut Nina out from the rest of the Seniors and tried by every means in their power to coax her to forgive Hilda. Nina remained implacable and, in despair, Mary-Lou had gone to the Head and begged leave to go to Freudesheim as she wanted to see Aunt Joey about "something frightfully important—and it *is* frightful, too," she had added consideringly.

Miss Annersley asked no questions though she guessed what was behind the request. She gave leave at once—the more readily because she herself had had a session with Nina after Frühstück and had made no greater impression on her than the girls had. Nina could see only her own point of view. She had no pity for Hilda's real unhappiness and all the Head could get out of her was a sullen, "It serves her right if she's miserable. She was warned and she didn't bother to remember. I can't practise and I couldn't have my lesson this morning."

"There are more important things than music, even," Miss Annersley said sternly. "I hope, until you feel differently about Hilda, you won't try to say Our Father, Nina. Have you ever thought what a terrible condemnation of yourself you are calling down if you ask to be forgiven your trespasses exactly as you forgive those of others? Think that over, please, and ask God to give you the grace of pity."

Nina had looked rather startled, but she said nothing and the Head had dismissed her with a heavy heart. She had almost decided to consult Joey herself, for if Hilda was miserable, Nina was no better, to judge by her looks. So she had instantly gone to ring up Freudesheim and returned to give Mary-Lou permission to wrap up and run across provided she was back within an hour. Mittagessen was to be early today and the girls were to have a long afternoon out-of-doors, tobogganing and ski-ing.

Mary-Lou had skipped across and poured out the whole story to Joey. Now she said anxiously, "But what can we *do* about it, Auntie Jo? Hilda's awfully miserable and," she added with a flash of insight that Joey had hardly expected of even her, "so is Nina. It can't be let go on, you know."

"Your English!" Joey said. Then, "It's no use going on at Nina. You'll only make her dig her toes in more. The best thing *you* can do is to pray for her. But Mary-Lou, there *is* something to be said for her. Try to understand a little."

"I can see that she had every reason to be mad at first," Mary-Lou replied. "But she's gone *on* being mad and that's what I don't understand."

"You can try. Listen to me. Do you remember last term after your accident when you first roused up and thought for some days that you might never walk again?"

Mary-Lou stared at her with parted lips. "I do, of course. I don't think I could ever forget. But," she added, "it didn't make me *hate* Emerence."

"Although it was really all her fault. I wasn't thinking of that side of it exactly but as you've brought it up, I'd just like to point out that you find it easy to forgive and Nina obviously doesn't. What I *was* getting at was how you felt until you knew that it would be all right sooner or later."

The blue eyes darkened at the memory. "I felt simply *awful!*"

"Yes; well, that's how Nina is feeling just now about her wrist."

"Auntie Joey, she simply *can't!*" She's known from the first that it was only a few days before she was all right again. I didn't—or not at first."

"Didn't you feel *sick* to get up and move about sometimes?" Joey asked.

"I did, of course." Mary-Lou paused. Then she said suddenly, "I'll tell you. There was one day when

I felt if I had to lie there a moment longer I must scream and scream and *scream!* I wanted almost maddeningly to get up and go flying around as I've always done. It seemed to me that if I had to lie like that for the rest of my life I'd go completely crackers. In fact, I rather hoped I'd die if it meant that."

"Nina is longing to be at her music in just that way," Joey said; and left it at that.

"But that's mad! She'll be at it again by the middle of next week at latest. It wasn't a really bad wrench, you know, though it did hurt. Must have done, for she was as white as chalk when we'd hauled Hilda off her."

"Don't you think Nina may have been terrified in case the damage was really bad? To be a concert pianist, your hands and wrists and arms must be perfect. Shall I tell you how it looks to me?"

"I wish you would! I quite like the kid, you know," said Mary-Lou, sublimely ignoring the fact that "the kid" was a bare three weeks younger than herself. "And, of course, we're all fond enough of poor old Hilda and *she's* a long, wet week over it all. You see, everyone went for her about it, because Miss Burnett did warn her twice about being careful. So what with that and knowing that the whole thing was her fault and Nina saying she won't have anything to do with her, Hilda's on the verge of weeps half the time. And we honestly don't know what to do about it."

"I've told you the best and only thing you can do. However, what strikes me is that for the first hour or so, Nina really did think her career was done in," said Joey cheerfully forgetting that she was a grown-up, the mother of a long family and a well-known writer, and reverting to schoolgirl language. "Well, she's had a series of quite nasty shocks in the past two months and she wasn't able to take it. She lost her father when he plunged into Maggiore to try to save a kid that had fallen in. She was whisked off to England by her guardian who is a very nice man—I met him when he came to fix her up at the Chalet School—but I should think that his high light in music is Handel's *Largo* and *perhaps* the *Moonlight*. At any rate, I'm certain he hasn't the foggiest notion how Nina feels. In fact, I doubt if any of his family has. Then, after never being at school but just living round with her father, she was plunged headlong into a very fair-sized one and she hasn't had anything like time to feel her feet yet. Her mind must be a whole jumble of muddled impressions and she can't sort them out. It's a pity Hilda made such an ass of herself, but you other people have *got* to be patient with Nina and do your best for her. Let the subject alone altogether in future. Keep her occupied with other ideas and don't give her a chance to brood on it."

"Then what happens to her mind if it's in a jumble to start with?" Mary-Lou demanded.

"Your ideas will be on the surface. Deep down inside I *hope* things will begin to straighten themselves out a little. But nothing you crowd can say will do it, so ignore it. That's my advice. She's coming to tea with me tomorrow and if I find I can do anything, I will. But I won't promise. I may decide that *I* should leave it alone, too. Now your hour is up and you must go. Before I forget, you can ask leave to come along on Sunday week. I must get all my parties over during this half of the term. After that, I shan't be able to manage."

Mary-Lou flashed her a look and she laughed. "Oh, I'm all right. Don't you start to worry about me. But

I'd like a few weeks of peace and quiet just then. That's all."

"Well, thanks a million," Mary-Lou said, getting up from her lowly seat on a hassock. I feel better about things now. I'll tell our crowd what you say and try to get the rest to lay off Nina. Perhaps," hopefully, "when she can play again she'll come round and forgive Hilda."

"I fully expect she will—if she doesn't forget all about it. Don't forget what I said about genius. It isn't selfishness in the ordinary sense. It's just that music means more to her than everything else put together. Only, for her own sake, she must learn to live with other people."

"Are all geniuses like that?" Mary-Lou asked as she pulled on her coat.

"It's a very common habit with them—though Bach, at any rate, must have been able to manage music *and* other folk. He had twenty children and married twice!"

"Gosh! He was worse than you?" cried the candid Mary-Lou.

"What on earth do you mean? I've only eight, so far! *And* one husband!"

Mary-Lou giggled. "I don't suppose you'll ever want more than the one husband. You'd have a ghastly time finding anyone else as nice as Uncle Jack! But about the family I wouldn't be so sure. I can just see you with a string of infants coming along for years to come!" She turned and fled to the door after this piece of impertinence and Joey giggled herself.

"You deserve to have your ears well boxed for that! However, I'll let it pass. Off you go or someone will have something to say to you. It's after twelve now."

Mary-Lou gave a shriek of horror and sped off as fast as she could go. Luckily, she had put on her nailed boots or she would have floundered all over for the ground was like glass. But she kept her balance and as Joey's clock was five minutes fast, she was able to join her fellows in the commonroom at St. Clare's just before the bell rang for Mittagessen.

"What luck?" Vi muttered as they lined up at the door.

"Tell you later. But Aunt Joey says we've got to lay off Nina, so we'll have to get at the rest on that point. There's second bell!" And Mary-Lou firmly held her tongue until they were all sitting down when she equally firmly changed the subject to the afternoon's sport and no more was said for the present.

Chapter IX

JOEY PUTS A FINGER IN THE PIE

NINA duly went to have "English Tea" with Mrs. Maynard on the Sunday. She was escorted to Freudesheim, the Maynard's house, by Len, the eldest of the family, who ushered her into the big salon with the words, "This is Nina, Mamma. Sorry I can't stop, but we three are booked for coffee with Auntie Biddy. Everyone quite fit?"

Mrs. Maynard was sitting by the french window which led into the garden. She turned to give her first-born a grin before she held out a welcoming hand to Nina. "Welcome to Freudesheim, Nina."

Nina flushed. "Thank you," she said shyly.

Len nodded to her. "You'll be all right now," she said. "I must scram. Con and Margot are waiting for me." She beamed at her mother and then fled, leaving Nina to make her own way with Joey.

"Come and take off your things," Mrs. Maynard said. "Then we must settle down for a good natter. You're admiring my piano," she added as she saw the route Nina's eyes took across the room. The salon at Freudesheim had been the original salon when the house was a guesthouse and had been used for dances and receptions. Joey had turned it into a delightful drawing-room. The parquet floor was gay with a scatter of rugs of many colours. In the fireplace, where originally there had been a big stove, was an open grate where logs burned merrily, casting rosy lights round about. The furniture was, to quote Joey herself, a mixed bag. From the English home had come chairs and tables, many of them antiques. A great settee stood to one side of the hearth; to the other was a table loaded with books and beside it a big armchair. There were chairs in the french window for people who wanted to enjoy the glorious view of the Jungfrau and at one side of the room was the Bechstein which had drawn Nina's gaze. Behind it was a big rosewood cabinet on the shelves of which were piles of sheet music. In a niche further along the wall was a china cabinet filled with porcelain, much of it museum pieces, glowing with colour. At the opposite side were long low shelves, crammed with books of every kind. The pictures on the walls were mainly prints, copies of Dutch still-life and landscapes. Stands holding flowering plants added to the charm of the room. Nina thought that she had never seen one that appealed to her more.

As for her hostess, she had fallen in love with her at once. The delicate oval face with its well-cut features, the beautiful black eyes that were giving her such friendly looks from beneath the deep fringe of black hair which crossed the broad brow to finish in great flat whorls of plaits on either side of her head, but above all the friendly look which explained to Nina why the whole school seemed to think so much of Mrs. Maynard, appealed to Nina intensely.

As for Joey, she took one look at the slim girl and realised that this was going to be no easy matter.

"Thank goodness for someone who will give the piano a little work, even if it's only scales and exercises," she said when they were settled in the salon. "I'm up to the eyes in work and family myself. I'll be deeply grateful to you if you'll give the poor thing a little regular work."

"Scales and exercises are about all I can give it for the next few weeks," Nina said ruefully. "You've heard what's happened to my wrist, haven't you, Mrs. Maynard?"

Joey nodded. "I heard. It's hard luck, of course, but it might have been a lot worse. And after all, Nina, trying as it is for you, it's a lot worse for Hilda. After all, it's mainly her fault and that's a ghastly feeling to have. Poor old Hilda. She's blaming herself bitterly, I hear."

Nina's face hardened. "She only *has* herself to blame. Three people did warn her about pressing down but she took no notice. It's no thanks to her that the damage isn't worse. My wrist might have been broken."

"Mercifully, it wasn't," Joey said. "That *would* have been a tragedy. Look on the bright side, Nina, and be grateful for mercies. And if you get a chance, do try to make Hilda see that point as well. If I know anything of that young woman, she's fretting herself into fiddlestrings about the business."

Nina turned startled eyes on her. "What on earth do you mean?" she demanded, forgetting the respect due to elders.

"What I say. Oh, come, Nina, use your imagination. Put yourself in Hilda's place. How would you feel?" Joey looked into Nina's eyes. "Hilda won't be happy again until she's heard you say you forgive her."

"Indeed?" There was a grimness in the rejoinder which warned Joey that it wasn't going to be as easy as all that. She ignored it and continued, "Now how can we fix it so that she can apologise naturally?"

"Don't worry. I don't want her apologies."

"That may be all very well from your point of view but you've got to consider Hilda's as well."

"I see no reason for it. Thanks to her I've missed hours and hours of practice and it matters."

"So does Hilda's happiness."

"She ought to have thought of that sooner."

Joey gave her a curious look. "Do you really feel that way?"

"How else would you expect me to feel?" Nina asked.

"Oh, raging at first. But I'd have got over it by this."

Nina looked at her. "Do you mean that:"

"Of course I do. It's not worth while holding on to any grudge. What good will it do you or anyone else? Far better forget all about it and give your time and thought to your work. And here comes tea!" she added as the sound of rattling china and trolley wheels came to them. "I hope you're ready for it. I am, I know." She laughed. "It always seems to me the most typically English meal of the lot when properly done. And it is today—teacakes—scones—thin bread-and-butter, fruitcake and Swiss pastries just to give a finish to everything."

Nina laughed. "It sounds awfully satisfying." But she gave Joey a wary look. What had this chat about tea to do with the trouble about Hilda?

Joey made no further comment. She turned to smile on the stout bespectacled maid in her trim uniform of dark blue print with white collar and cuffs who wheeled in the well-laden tea trolley and placed it before her mistress.

"Thank you, Anna," Joey said. She bestowed a smile on the maid, who gave her mistress a beaming grin in return before she departed.

"Anna," said Joey as she proceeded to pour out tea, "is my great stand-by. She has been with me since

106

I married. There was a time when we thought we were going to lose her to quite a nice young man, but when it came to the point she decided that I needed her more than he did and certainly couldn't manage without her, so she gave him the brush-off. In one way I was sorry. She would have made a splendid wife and mother. Actually, I think she didn't really care for him—not in the right way. Never forget, Nina, that while you may have various fancies the real test is whether you love a man whatever his moods and whims may be, and whether he comes first and foremost with you no matter what. Anyhow, I have no complaints, seeing how we have benefitted by her decision. She bosses the family and seems completely happy about it. Here's your tea—and try a teacake. Anna bakes them to perfection. She learned the art when we were living in England."

Nothing more was said about Hilda and the accident until tea was over and Anna had wheeled the trolley back to the kitchen. Then Joey drew Nina over to the long window at the end of the salon.

"Nina," she said, "look at the mountains." Nina obediently gazed out of the window. "Look at the size of them. When I consider them like this I am always struck with the *bigness* of them—how small we and our affairs are in comparison."

Nina gazed out at the great masses opposite. "I never thought of them that way," she said slowly, "but I see what you mean, Mrs. Maynard."

"Good! And will you see what I mean when I say that when we live with other people we have to think of their side of things occasionally?"

It was impossible for Nina to go redder, but she forced herself to look up into Joey's face. "You mean——"

107

Joey nodded. "Exactly. You've let your side of this silly accident so overwhelm you that you've had neither time nor room to think that there's Hilda's side to it as well as yours. Think of it now. She's had the worst of it, after all. I know you've had the aching to put up with; also you were afraid of real damage to your wrist for a short while, but that is all. Now think of Hilda's share. The whole thing was her fault and she knows it. To make matters worse, she was warned over and over again and then forgot. She's been told about that by at least three people, not to mention all her own crowd have had to say on the subject. Hilda may be careless and featherheaded, but she has a hefty conscience and that hasn't given her much peace. She's done all she can in the way of apology, but you've refused to accept it."

Nina crimsoned again. "I—I——"

"Yes; I thought you'd see it if it was pointed out to you," Joey said. "You get hold of her and tell her so at the first opportunity. And do try to remember that you're supposed to be a Christian and behave in a Christian way. Now come and meet our noble hound. Do you like dogs, Nina?"

"Very much indeed, though I've never had one of my own. You can't when you're moving about all the time. What kind of dog is yours?"

"A St. Bernard." Joey picked up a photograph from the top of the bookcase. "That's my precious Rufus." Something in her voice told Nina that "precious" was the operative word. Joey looked at her and then went on. "He died of old age some years ago and I just couldn't bear to have another dog for some time. Then the school presented me with Bruno and he's going strong I can tell you. He's out of puppyhood, but he retains several puppy tricks. For example, he greets visitors with much vim, so stand by to repell boarders." Just then a large white and golden gentleman came bursting through a communicating door from the next room and bounced joyously at his mistress. His onset was quite unexpected by Nina who yelled again with surprise, but it put a definite end to any resentment she might have been feeling, and a little later, before she went back to the school, she looked up into Joey's face and said, "I'm sorry I've been such a beast to Hilda and—and I'll tell her so."

"Oh, good egg!" Joey spoke with enthusiasm. "I thought you were too decent at bottom to keep up an undying feud like that. And now we can look forward to the pantomime without a shadow on anything."

Chapter X

"BEAUTY AND THE BEAST"

WHEN Nina returned from Freudesheim the first thing she did was to hunt out Hilda who had cheered up a little by this time.

"Hilda," she said shame-facedly, "I'm so very sorry I was so unkind to you. Please forgive me if you can."

This took place in the splashery where Hilda coming for a drink of water, had encountered Nina in the act of hanging up her coat. Being Hilda, she held out her hand at once. "Of course I will! And will you forgive me for being such an ass? Miss Lawrence told me I might have injured your wrist permanently and that would have been simply ghastly."

As a result, the startled members of Va beheld the pair coming into the formroom together and if Hilda looked her old happy self, Nina had certainly lost her brooding look. By Wednesday, her arm was out of the sling and Dr. Graves gave her permission to practise with the left hand for ten minutes at a time. The wrist remained weak for some days, but by the time February was half over, Nina was taking her full four hours a day. More than that, she was gaining in colour and weight and seemed to have settled down happily.

The thing that occupied most minds by then was the St. Mildred pantomime.

The girls had elected to produce *Beauty and the Beast* and they had roped in a goodly number of the school proper as they wanted to make a really big thing of it. Verity Carey, Mary-Lou's "sister-by-marriage," since Commander Carey had married Mrs. Trelawney, was the Fairy Queen. The whole bunch of prefects with the exception of Betsy Lucy were Robin Hood and his Merry Men. Betsy herself was Puck. Others of the elder girls were servants, messengers, palace guards and other oddments. Seventeen people who knew something about ballet had been handed over to Tatiana Khavasky whose aunt was, to quote Margot Maynard, "a *real* ballet dancer," and the younger folk were fairies, elves, pixies, and goblins. The chief characters were, naturally, in the hands of the St. Mildred girls. Julie Lucy, sister of Betsy and Vi, was the Beast and her Beauty was an extremely pretty girl who had come from another school, one Joy Venn. Big Ruth Wilson was the Merchant and his elder daughters were Dorothy Watson and Polly Winterton, also Chalet School girls. Clem Barras, another Chaletian, was the Wicked Fairy, having laid claim to it from the beginning, and Annis Lovell, a friend of hers, was the Boatman who suffered from spoonerisms. A big girl from Carnbach Grammar School was the Coachman and the last word in pomposity. The Horse was composed of Bride Bettany and a girl from a Brighton school, Mary Elliot.

The pantomime came off in the afternoon. It was necessary to make a matinée of it since part of the audience might not be out after dark, even though the place was the hall built by subscription from various friends just beyond the gates of the Sanatorium. It began at fourteen o'clock—two, in English time—and by half past thirteen, the body of the hall was crowded. Sundry people from the main school were very busy acting as doorkeepers and usherettes and during the second interval, coffee and cakes were to

111

be provided at a moderate sum. As Bride Bettany had remarked, "We want to make all we can for the San, as well as giving them a lot of fun."

There was resounding applause when the orchestra, made up of pupils of all the school, filed in and took their places. Nina had been requested to take over the piano from Miss Lawrence so was among them to her great delight.

When Mr. Denny arrived to take possession of the conductor's rostrum, there was a second outburst. It died away as his baton was raised, bows came to the ready and Nina, with her eyes fixed on him, touched the keys lovingly. Then the baton came down and they swung into Nicolai's *Merry Wives of Windsor* overture which they had calmly pitched on for the purpose.

The final chords crashed out and after the applause which the conductor acknowledged with three jerky bows, he turned back, the opening chorus sounded and the curtains swept up, showing "The hall in the house of Master Geltibran, a rich merchant." The servants were scuttling about, getting into each other's way, and the Boatman appeared with a couple of stuffed fish to announce solemnly that he had brought "two hied drerring" for his master's refreshment on his journey—which brought the first laugh. The Merchant appeared, gorgeous in crimson and green, together with his three daughters, Adeliza, Mariella and Beauty, the first two in elaborate dresses and the last in a gym tunic with her hair tied back. Her sisters kept crowding her out and calling her "child," despite her complaints that she was nineteen and surely might be considered grown-up now. Master Geltibran promised the gifts and the elder sisters sneered at Beauty's modest request for a rose. Then there was a cry of, "Way! Make way there!" and the Coachman arrived, leading the Merchant's horse in.

The animal proceeded to display antics that would have caused any ordinary steed to be sold to the nearest circus. It had movable eyelids of enormous size and it winked solemnly at its master before it administered a side kick at the Coachman who got out of the way in such a hurry that he fell over a page and the pair went down. While the crowd were still rocking, the beast sidled up to a chair which the Merchant mounted, but when he tried to get on its back, it turned, cocked its head on one side and winked at him, pawing valiantly while the audience rocked again.

At long last he managed to get there and the Horse moved off. The audience were not to know that as Ruth's weight descended, the hindquarters gasped, "Gosh! What a ton-weight! Thank goodness it's only into the wings!" As a result, the gentleman nearly forgot to wave to his family as they clattered off, the Merchant grinning broadly. Beauty wept gracefully into her handkerchief, but Adeliza yelled, "Whatever you do, don't forget my diamond tiara and necklace!" which had been her modest request! Mariella, not to be outdone, bawled a reminder of the dozen dresses from Paris she had ordered. The scene ended with a sung farewell during which the servants poured on to the stage in such numbers that Joey Maynard, sitting next to Miss Wilson and Miss Annersley, was moved to murmur, "Labour must have been cheap then!"

The next scene took place before a front-cloth and was the Merchant's house. The Cook was busy with the dinner and in reply to every question asked merely replied, "Pepper it!" The climax came when a kitchen-maid plaintively asked how she should deal with the rice pudding ordered by Adeliza for Beauty and was told, "Pepper it!" which drew shouts of laughter from the audience. Worse was to come, however, for the Boatman arrived to ask if he could take any people to parket. He complained that he could do with a tup of kea and asked if Cook had any cruffins or mumpets. At this point, Miss Annersley moaned gently and Joey mopped her streaming eyes with her programme as her handkerchief seemed to have gone missing!

By way of contrast, the next scene was the Court of the Fairy Queen which opened with a chorus which was a very old song indeed, *The Fairies*, produced by Joey who had begged, borrowed or stolen all she could find for the purpose. This was followed by a charming dance given by the ballet. Then the Fairy Queen sang the story of the spell laid on Prince Charming by the Wicked Fairy, Nettlesting, and which could only be broken by a maiden as good as she was beautiful who loved the Beast with all her heart.

Verity had a beautiful voice, with a lark's lilt in it, and fully deserved the applause she received. However, no encores could be allowed, so the orchestra swung into a merry round dance and the little fairyfolk skipped and pranced gaily.

Into this happy scene erupted Nettlesting. Clem looked really dreadful. She had "back-combed" her whole red-brown mop until it stood on end above her face and over her shoulders. She had given herself a ferocious scowl and, someone having fatally introduced her to nose-paste, had adorned her own pretty nose with a hump in the middle.

Joey sat up and surveyed her with interest. "Heavens!- How could Clem manage to make herself so ghastly?" she queried in tones that carried up to the stage and nearly gave Nettlesting a fit of the giggles.

However, she controlled herself, raised the crooked stick she was carrying and bellowed that the Queen would never lift the spell for no such girl existed. So defiant were her words and gestures that Verity, usually no actress, was roused to make her reply with real dramatic fervour, much to the relief of the producer, Miss Wilson, who had frequently moaned over the flat gentleness of her words during rehearsal. Nettlesting defied her and the Queen told her rebellious subject that when the spell was broken, the Wicked Fairy would be banished to the Land of the Green Goblins forever, whereupon, the Green Goblins, whose faces looked simply awful, done with green greasepaint, suddenly came tumbling in and hailed Nettlesting as their future queen in a song whose chorus ran,

> "Pinch her, nip her,
>   Hit her with a slipper!
>   Turn her in reverse!
>   Drive her in a hearse!
> And show her what our queen will meet
> When she comes to Green Goblin Land!"

All the time, they were tumbling about, turning somersaults and cartwheels until one visitor muttered to her next door neighbour that those children must be made of indiarubber! With a final shriek of rage, Nettlesting strode off, her future subjects tumbling after her. The ballet took the stage with a graceful dance to a Chopin valse and the curtains came down to rise a minute or two later on a front-cloth scene between the Merchant, the Coachman and the Horse.

Once more the audience were reduced to helpless laughter as the Merchant bemoaned his ill-luck in the matter of the rose and berated the Coachman for not finding him any. The Coachman, speaking in words of three or four syllables, pointed out that you couldn't expect to find roses growing in the Muscovy plains in the middle of winter. The Horse suddenly kicked out at him with a playful hind hoof, and then proceeded to chase him round the stage to the tune of a wild rondo from the orchestra while the Merchant, hurriedly mounting a log handily at one side, encouraged his steed, ejaculating, "Good old Dobbin! Keep it up, old boy! Move a bit faster, Consequential, or he'll dot you one!. *Got* him!" as the Horse contacted the Coachman's hindquarters, rather harder than was meant and the yell that gentleman let out was genuine! Finally. the three careered off and the curtains fell once more.

They rose again on the Garden of the Beast's Palace. The girls had spent a good deal of effort and ingenuity on this. Paper roses trailed over the painted canvas walls and about a trellised archway. Rose-bushes had been contrived out of them and branches of fir with quite good if somewhat unusual effect. In the middle of the stage rose a cardboard fountain, the water being effected by means of strands of fine silver wire curved over gracefully into the bowl. A garden seat from St. Mildred's stood at one side and hither came the Merchant who seemed to have mislaid his Horse for the time being. He dropped on to the seat and gave way to a long soliloquy during which he proclaimed that though he had sought everywhere, he could not find the rose Beauty wanted. Towards the

116

end of his speech, the orchestra began playing a lullaby pianissimo. He yawned and then stretched himself out on the seat with one of the parcels for a pillow and the ballet drifted in in a dreamy dance performed mainly down front so that very few people could see the small fairies carefully wheeling in a table already laid and drawing it up beside the sleeping gentleman. The music modulated into the lovely old English lullaby, *Golden Slumbers*, while the ballet melted into the wings with the fairies and as it ended, the Merchant roused up, rubbed his eyes, saw the table with many ejaculations and rubbed them again.

He finally sat up and after lifting the covers and remarking on each dish, helped himself and fell to. When he had eaten, he looked round and woke up to the fact that he was in a rose garden. He wandered round it, rhapsodizing all the time and finally plucked a rose. There was a terrific *"Crash!"* and the Beast stood beside him, growling most alarmingly. The Merchant fell on his knees and begged for mercy. The Beast growled again and a band of soldiers, gorgeous in red and gold, marched in and surrounded the trespasser. The Merchant shrieked—and little wonder. The Beast was an awesome-looking creature, clad in a teddy-bear suit that covered him from chin to toes and with a head on him that no animal in the Zoo had ever produced. He advanced on the stricken man and at this point, an entirely unrehearsed effect occurred.

Joey had been obliged to bring her twins to the show as she wanted everyone in the house to share the fun. Felix and Felicity, the two-and-a-half-year-old twins, had watched everything with wide blue eyes, gurgling when the grown-ups laughed and otherwise behaving beautifully. But this was where Felix, staring at the queer creature on the stage, suddenly exclaimed

117

in bell-like tones, "Oh! *Funny* doggy! Wants to stwoke ve funny doggy, Mamma!"

"You can't! Sit still!" Joey hissed, leaning over to hold him down, while the Merchant uttered a remark that sounded like "Pup-chick!" and the Beast made a most peculiar sound.

The girls were well-drilled, however, and the Beast recovered himself at once and proceeded to demand why his hospitality had been so abused. The Merchant, in very wobbly tones, explained and the well-known condition for his release was uttered. The Merchant promised and was led off into the palace while the ballet danced in and the scene ended.

There was a brief interval, during which Joey impressed on her youngest pair that they must sit quietly. Then the curtain rose on the Merchant's front hall again and he arrived and told his story. The elder sisters complained when they heard that Beauty was to marry the Beast and own the beautiful palace. Their father told them it was their own fault for being so greedy and a very funny scene took place which ended with the Horse arriving to bear Beauty away and gallumphing off in a highly upsetting manner for its rider who nearly fell from it before it reached the wings.

A drop scene of a river when the Boatman, the Cook, the Coachman and the ubiquitous Horse fooled excellently, gave the perspiring scene-shifters a chance to set the Throne Room of the palace. They were just ready when an entirely unexpected event happened.

Tht Horse had tried to kiss the Cook. Every time he stretched out his neck in her direction, she shrieked and ran. The audience were mopping their eyes and screaming with laughter, when the hindquarters tripped, bunted into the back of the forequarters

118

which was not expecting it and staggered forward, tripped over the Coachman and the latter went down, fell flat, the back legs subsiding on top of him and the forelegs sitting on top of the back legs.

The audience merely wept—it was about all they could do by this time. As for the orchestra which was supposed to keep up an undercurrent of music here, the members were doubled up over their instruments and it was reported later that Nina simply laid her head on the piano keys and shook with laughter. Even Mr. Denny—Plato to his pupils—dropped his baton and leaned on the desk and writhed with mirth.

Luckily for the pantomime, Adeliza and Mariella kept their heads. They had been in the wings, waiting for their next entrance and they rushed on to the stage, Adeliza hissing at all within hearing, "Gag till we can straighten up!" before she and Mariella hauled the horse off the unfortunate Coachman who was nearly purple under his greasepaint by the time they got him on his legs again. Indeed, Adeliza deserved a medal for presence of mind for she raved at everyone in an impromptu speech which fitted in so well, that quite half the visitors thought it was all part of the act.

The next scene showed the arrival of the wedding party in the Throne Room. For no known reason, Adeliza swept in on the arm of Little John and Mariella arrived with Robin Hood. The outlaw band sang a chorus extolling the glories of a free forest life and followed this up with the old Morris dance, *How D'Ye Do, Sir?*

The music then modulated into *Haste to the Wedding* and Beauty arrived, all in white and complete with veil and bouquet, what time the Beast entered from the other side, supported by the Captain of the Guard and the entire Guard. A quartette followed between Beauty, the Beast, the Merchant and the Captain, after which the entire party danced a charming minuet before going out to supper.

As the last of the party vanished, the stage darkened and Nettlesting and her retinue appeared. Standing well down centre, Nettlesting, lighted by a green lime which made her look even more awful if that were possible, solemnly cursed the happy pair with a most comprehensive curse.

> "May their stockings hole and ladder;
> Each day may the pair grow madder;
> May their wit be met with squashing;
> May the laundries rip their washing.
> May their teeth be always aching;
> May their window-cords keep breaking;
> May their orders be forgotten;
> May their eggs be always rotten;
> May their television wobble;
> With great chilblains may they hobble;
> May corns grow on all their toeses;
> Streaming colds afflict their noses;
> May the soot choke up their flues;
> Transmission faults break in on news;
> May their milk turn every morning;
> Horrid dreams from dusk till dawning
> Haunt their sleep; may he grow bald;
> May she turn into a scold.
> May their brats be cross-eyed, bandy,
> Screaming all the time for candy;
> May the palace woodwork splinter;
> May their pipes burst every winter;
> Last and worst thing to befall,
> May they never laugh at all!"

Having shrieked out this verse in a falsetto voice that made Jack Maynard mutter to his friend Dr. Graves, "If Clem doesn't want a gargle after all this, I miss my guess!" Nettlesting broke into a series of shrill cackles which were nearly ruined by a small voice from the audience proclaiming, "Ooh! Isn't Clem *funny!*" Joey's third son, Michael, was giving tongue for the benefit of the twins in case they were frightened.

If thoughts could have killed, Mike would have been slain. Clem glared out across the auditorium, but in any case, the audience were shaking at the funny mixture of horrors and the next moment, amber limes brought on the Fairy Queen who dared Nettlesting to carry out any of her curses.

The bad fairy cried that though the pair were wedded, Beauty had no love of her husband and never would and the spell would remain.

"Not so, for she is good as she is beautiful and one day your wicked spell will end, for love will have vanquished it," the Queen retorted.

The orchestra struck up and she sang a charming lyric in praise of love while Nettlesting shrank away and the Queen was left, standing in the limelight as the curtains slowly whispered down.

The second interval occurred here and trays of coffee and cakes were passed along the rows of seats. In fact, so great was the demand, that Matron at the Sanatorium had to send one of the nurses to bring all the staff's spare cups.

"I need this!" Joey said as she sipped hers. "*What* a show! I wonder who was responsible for the Curse? I call it most comprehensive!"

. "So do I," Miss Wilson agreed. "I believe Bride Bettany wrote it—with some help from the rest. I know there's a lot more of it, but they cut it down because of the time. What a relish that bad Clem used on it!"

"What awful doggerel!" retorted Miss Annersley. "I must set them all to sonnet-writing next time I take them for English. Finished, Joey? Then pass your cup along. Emerence is waiting for it."

Joey handed over the empty cup and then leaned forward to address her young who sat just in front. "Once more and for the last time," she said severely, *"you are not to talk!* If you do that again, I'll take you all home! Then you'll miss all the end of it. You two boys are awful! Felicity's the only one who's behaved herself properly so far. All right, Felicity? Have you finished your sweets?"

"No, sank you," Felicity said with a beaming smile at her mother.

"Well but, Mamma, I was only afraid the kids might be frightened," Mike objected.

"Not they! They've seen too many of the shows you folk get up in the holidays," his mother said. "Anyhow, if you do it again, you know what will happen—*all* of you!"

As Joey always did as she said, she had secured silence from them for the rest of the pantomime and as the orchestra struck up again at that moment and the footlights suddenly blazed up, she sat back and the pantomime continued.

Scene followed scene. Beauty was summoned home and she and the Beast had quite a pathetic duet before she finally went off on the back of the Horse which had recovered from the shock of its last mishap.

The next scene was the welcome given Beauty who arrived loaded with gifts for all and sundry. The Boatman had the audience laughing again as he thanked "Princess Beauty" for the "tound of pobacco and the priar bipe" she had brought him, and Adeliza and Mariella who were now wedded to the Captain of the Guard and Robin Hood compared notes on their gifts and quarrelled as to who had the best.

Next came the scene where Beauty tells of her dream that the Beast wants her. She sang very prettily of his love for her and how fond of him she had grown, while her sisters did their best to dissuade her from going, turning aside to apply stage onions to their eyes, drawing her attention to their tears after each application. Nettlesting appeared from the wings, watching the scene with gloating asides. The Fairy Queen came opposite and a chorus, sung pianissimo by the fairies, reminded Beauty of her promise. She nearly yielded. Then she suddenly broke away from the exulting and envious sisters.

'He wants me—he needs me! And I love him!" she cried.

Exit Nettlesting, shaking clenched fists above her head, while the fairy chorus swelled out triumphantly!

This scene had been acted before the kitchen frontcloth, so there was no pause and the curtains rose on the final scene of all—the Beast's garden where he lay at the foot of the fountain, evidently in a parlous state. Beauty came rushing in, calling him. She found him and flung herself down beside him, spreading her arms about him to hide the fact that he was pulling down the zip fastening of his teddy-bear garment. Nettlesting appeared behind the fountain in one last effort to save her spell, but as Beauty cried, "Oh, Beast! My own dear Beast! Don't die! Stay with me, for I love you so much and I can't live without you!" the blue limes which had flooded the stage changed to amber and rose; the orchestra broke

123

into triumphal music; the fairies and their Queen flocked on to the stage and the Prince in all the glory of a golden suit rose and helped Beauty to her feet before taking her into his arms. The fairies sang a joyful song and Nettlesting with a noise that sounded likt "G—r—r—r!" turned and fled.

This was almost the end. The various characters came crowding on as Prince Charming led his bride up the steps to the palace entrance and they stood there under a rose-arch which had been rushed into position during the earlier scene. The orchestra swung into the *Bridal March* from *Lohengrin* and the entire band sang:

> "Ring out, ye bells,
> Joyous and sweet!
> Happy the pair that we welcome today!
> Glad be your lives,
> You whom we greet!
> Happiness dower ye both now and alway!
> Here 'mid the roses, love shall be yours.
> Here, ye shall know the joy that endures.
> Sing, brothers, sing!
> Raise the bright strain!
> True love has won! Join ye in our refrain!"

The music changed to Tchaikovsky's *Valse des Fleurs* and the Sylphs whirled into a mazy dance on which the curtains fell, only to be raised a minute later to show the Merchant joining the hands of Beauty and Prince Charming while the Fairy Queen, mounted just above them on a step-ladder in front of which the tall Guards stood to hide what it was, balanced with hands outspread in blessing on the happy pair. The rest of the company were grouped in charming tableaux and as the curtain rose, they sang their final chorus again before it fell and the music changed to *God Save The Queen* and the pantomime was over!

"Well, did you enjoy it?" asked Mary-Lou as she and Nina arrived in their dormitory.

Nina laughed. "*Very* much. It was great fun. I *am* glad I came to the Chalet School, Mary-Lou, and I'm looking forward tremendously to the rest of the term."

And Mary-Lou, looking at Nina's happy face, was satisfied. Nina would always put her music first, but Mary-Lou was sure that she was beginning to realise that people could also be worth studying.

"And I'll bet," thought Mary-Lou with a sudden flash of understanding, "that Auntie Joey would say the more she realises that, the better musician she'll become. Good old Nina! We'll be proud of her yet!"

The second part of
A Genius at the Chalet School
is published in Armada in
Chalet School Fête.

MILL GREEN

School Series

by *Alison Prince*

Now there's a great new school series in Armada.

Mill Green is a big, new comprehensive – with more than its fair share of dramas and disasters! Get to know Matt, Danny, Rachel, and the rest of the First Form mob in their first two exciting adventures.

Mill Green on Fire
When someone starts fires in the school and blames the caretaker, Matt is determined to catch the real culprit. But his brilliant plan to catch the firebug goes horribly wrong . . .

Mill Green on Stage
The First Formers prepare for the Christmas pantomime – and sparks soon fly when Marcia Mudd, a ghastly new girl, gets the best part. But when Matt locks Marcia in a cupboard and she disappears from the school, there's big trouble for everyone . . .

More stories about Mill Green will be published in Armada.

Armada

SUPERSLEUTHS

by FRANKLIN W. DIXON and CAROLYN KEENE

A feast of reading for all mystery fans!

At last, the Hardy Boys and Nancy Drew have joined forces to become the world's most brilliant detective team!

Together, the daredevil sleuths investigate seven spine-chilling mysteries: a deadly roller-coaster that hurtles to disaster, a sinister bell that tolls in a city of skeletons, a haunted opera house with a sinister curse — and many more terrifying situations.

Nancy Drew and the Hardy Boys — *dynamite!*

Armada

CAPTAIN ARMADA

HI KIDS!
I'VE GOT THE
POWER TO BRING YOU FUN,
ADVENTURE, AND
EXCITEMENT!

Here are just some of the best-selling titles that Armada has to offer:

- [ ] The Whizzkid's Handbook 2 Peter Eldin 95p
- [ ] The Vanishing Thieves Franklin W. Dixon 95p
- [ ] 14th Armada Ghost Book Mary Danby 85p
- [ ] The Chalet School and Richenda Elinor M. Brent-Dyer 95p
- [ ] The Even More Awful Joke Book Mary Danby 95p
- [ ] Adventure Stories Enid Blyton 85p
- [ ] Biggles Learns to Fly Captain W. E. Johns 90p
- [ ] The Mystery of Horseshoe Canyon Ann Sheldon 95p
- [ ] Mill Green on Stage Alison Prince 95p
- [ ] The Mystery of the Sinister Scarecrow Alfred Hitchcock 95p
- [ ] The Secret of Shadow Ranch Carolyn Keene 95p

Armadas are available in bookshops and newsagents, but can also be ordered by post.

HOW TO ORDER
ARMADA BOOKS, Cash Sales Dept., GPO Box 29, Douglas, Isle of Man, British Isles. Please send purchase price of book plus postage as follows:–

    1–4 Books .... 10p per copy
    5 Books or more . . . . no further charge
    25 Books sent post free within U.K.

Overseas Customers: 12p per copy

NAME (Block letters)

_____

ADDRESS

_____

_____

_____